A   REVIVED

MODERN

CLASSIC

LAUGHTER IN THE DARK

VLADIMIR NABOKOV

LAUGHTER IN
THE DARK

A NEW DIRECTIONS BOOK

Revised edition first published by New Directions in 1960; first issued as a New Directions Paperbook in 1978; published in 1991 as New Directions Paperbook 729 in the Revived Modern Classics Series.

Manufactured in the United States of America
New Directions Books are printed on acid-free paper
Published simultaneously in Canada by Penguin Books Canada Limited.

Library of Congress Cataloging-in-Publication Data

Nabokov, Vladimir Vladimirovich, 1899-1977.
   [Kamera obskura. English]
   Laughter in the dark / Vladimir Nabokov.
       p.   cm. — (A Revived modern classic)
   ISBN 0-8112-1186-X
   I. Title.   II. Series.
PG3476.N3K313   1991
891.73'42—dc20   91-18665
                                               CIP

New Directions Books are published for James Laughlin
by New Directions Publishing Corporation
80 Eighth Avenue, New York 10011

A   REVIVED

MODERN

CLASSIC

LAUGHTER IN THE DARK

⊷§ 1 §⊷

ONCE upon a time there lived in Berlin, Germany, a man called Albinus. He was rich, respectable, happy; one day he abandoned his wife for the sake of a youthful mistress; he loved; was not loved; and his life ended in disaster.

This is the whole of the story and we might have left it at that had there not been profit and pleasure in the telling; and although there is plenty of space on a gravestone to contain, bound in moss, the abridged version of a man's life, detail is always welcome.

It so happened that one night Albinus had a beautiful idea. True, it was not quite his own, as it had been suggested by a phrase in Conrad (not the famous Pole, but Udo Conrad who wrote the *Memoirs of a Forgetful Man* and that other thing about the old conjuror who spirited himself away at his farewell performance). In any case, he made it his own by liking it, playing with it, letting it grow upon him, and that goes to make lawful property in the free city of the mind. As an art critic and picture expert he had often amused himself by having this or that Old Master sign landscapes and faces which he, Albinus, came across in real life: it turned his existence into a fine picture gallery—delightful fakes, all of them. Then, one night, as he was giving his learned mind a holiday and writing a little essay (nothing very brilliant, he was not a particularly gifted man) upon the art of the cinema, the beautiful idea came to him.

It had to do with colored animated drawings —which had just begun to appear at the time. How fascinating it would be, he thought, if one could use this method for having some well-known picture, preferably of the Dutch School, perfectly reproduced on the screen in vivid colors and then brought to life—movement and gesture graphically developed in complete harmony with their static state in the picture; say, a pot-house with little people drinking lustily at wooden tables and a sunny glimpse of a courtyard with saddled horses—all suddenly coming to life with that little man in red putting down his tankard, this girl with the tray wrenching herself free, and a hen beginning to peck on the threshold. It could be continued by having the little figures

8

come out and then pass through the landscape of the same painter, with, perhaps, a brown sky and a frozen canal, and people on the quaint skates they used then, sliding about in the old-fashioned curves suggested by the picture; or a wet road in the mist and a couple of riders—finally, returning to the same tavern, little by little bringing the figures and light into the self-same order, settling them down, so to speak, and ending it all with the first picture. Then, too, you could try the Italians: the blue cone of a hill in the distance, a white looping path, little pilgrims winding their way upward. And even religious subjects perhaps, but only those with small figures. And the designer would not only have to possess a thorough knowledge of the given painter and his period, but be blessed with talent enough to avoid any clash between the movements produced and those fixed by the old master: he would have to work them out from the picture—oh, it could be done. And the colors . . . they would be sure to be far more sophisticated than those of animated cartoons. What a tale might be told, the tale of an artist's vision, the happy journey of eye and brush, and a world in that artist's manner suffused with the tints he himself had found!

After a while he happened to speak of it to

a film-producer, but the latter was not in the least excited: he said it would entail a delicacy of work calling for novel improvements in the method of animation, and would cost a whole lot of money; he said such a film, owing to its laborious designing, could not reasonably run longer than several minutes; that even then it would bore most people to death and be a general disappointment.

Then Albinus discussed it with another cinema man, and he too pooh-poohed the whole business. "We could begin by something quite simple," said Albinus, "a stained window coming to life, animated heraldry, a little saint or two."

"I'm afraid it's no good," said the other. "We can't risk fancy pictures."

But Albinus still clung to his idea. Eventually he was told of a clever fellow, Axel Rex, who was a wonderful hand at freaks—had, as a matter of fact, designed a Persian fairy tale which had delighted highbrows in Paris and ruined the man who had financed the venture. So Albinus tried to see him, but learned that he had just returned to the States, where he was drawing cartoons for an illustrated paper. After some time Albinus managed to get in touch with him and Rex seemed interested.

Upon a certain day in March Albinus got a

long letter from him, but its arrival coincided with a sudden crisis in Albinus' private—very private—life, so that the beautiful idea, which otherwise would have lingered on and perhaps found a wall on which to cling and blossom, had strangely faded and shriveled in the course of the last week.

Rex wrote that it was hopeless to go on trying to seduce the Hollywood people and coolly went on to suggest that Albinus, being a man of means, should finance his idea himself; in which case he, Rex, would accept a fee of so much (a startling sum), with half of it payable in advance, for designing say a Breughel film—the "Proverbs" for instance, or anything else Albinus might like to have him set in motion.

"If I were you," remarked Albinus' brother-in-law Paul, a stout good-natured man with the clasps of two pencils and two fountain pens edging his breast-pocket, "I should risk it. Ordinary films cost more—I mean those with wars and buildings crumpling up."

"Oh, but then you get it all back, and I shouldn't."

"I seem to recall," said Paul, puffing at his cigar (they were finishing supper), "that you proposed sacrificing a considerable amount—hardly less than the fee he requires. Why, what's the

11

matter? You don't look as enthusiastic as you were a little while ago. You aren't giving it up, are you?"

"Well, I don't know. It's the practical side that rather bothers me; otherwise I do still like my idea."

"What idea?" inquired Elisabeth.

That was a little habit of hers—asking questions about things that had already been exhaustively discussed in her presence. It was sheer nervousness on her part, not obtuseness or lack of attention; and more often than not while still asking her question, sliding helplessly down the sentence, she would herself realize that she knew the answer all the time. Her husband was aware of this little habit and it never annoyed him; on the contrary, it touched and amused him. He would calmly go on with the talk, well knowing (and rather looking forward to it) that presently she would supply the answer to her own question. But on this particular March day Albinus was in such a state of irritation, confusion, misery, that suddenly his nerves gave way.

"Just dropped from the moon?" he inquired roughly, and his wife glanced at her fingernails and said soothingly:

"Oh yes, I remember now."

Then turning to eight-year-old Irma who was

12

messily devouring a plateful of chocolate cream, she cried:

"Not so fast, dear, please, not so fast."

"I consider," began Paul, puffing at his cigar, "that every new invention—"

Albinus, his queer emotions riding him, thought: "What the devil do I care for this fellow Rex, this idiotic conversation, this chocolate cream . . . ? I'm going mad and nobody knows it. And I can't stop, it's hopeless trying, and tomorrow I'll go there again and sit like a fool in that darkness. . . . Incredible."

Certainly it was incredible—the more so as in all the nine years of his married life he had curbed himself, had never, never—"As a matter of fact," he thought, "I ought to tell Elisabeth about it; or just go away with her for a little while; or see a psychoanalyst; or else . . ."

No, you can't take a pistol and plug a girl you don't even know, simply because she attracts you.

❧ 2 ❧

A<small>LBINUS</small> had never been very lucky in affairs of the heart. Although he was good-looking, in a quiet well-bred way, he somehow failed to derive any practical benefit from his appeal to women—for there was decidedly something very appealing about his pleasant smile and the mild blue eyes which bulged a little when he was thinking hard (and as he had a slowish mind this occurred more often than it should). He was a good talker, with just that very slight hesitation in his speech, the best part of a stammer, which lends fresh charm to the stalest sentence. Last but not least (for he lived in a smug German world) he had been left a soundly invested fortune by his father; yet, still, romance had a trick of becoming flat when it came his way.

In his student days he had had a tedious liaison of the heavyweight variety with a sad elderly lady who later, during the War, had sent out to

14

him at the front purple socks, tickly woollies
and enormous passionate letters written at top
speed in a wild illegible hand on parchment paper.
Then there had been that affair with the Herr
Professor's wife met on the Rhine; she was pretty,
when viewed at a certain angle and in a certain
light, but so cold and coy that he soon gave her
up. Finally, in Berlin, just before his marriage,
there had been a lean dreary woman with a
homely face who used to come every Saturday
night and was wont to relate all her past in detail, repeating the same damned thing over and
over again, sighing wearily in his embraces and
always rounding off with the one French phrase
she knew: "*C'est la vie.*" Blunders, gropings, disappointment; surely the Cupid serving him was
lefthanded, with a weak chin and no imagination. And alongside of these feeble romances
there had been hundreds of girls of whom he had
dreamed but whom he had never got to know;
they had just slid past him, leaving for a day or
two that hopeless sense of loss which makes
beauty what it is: a distant lone tree against
golden heavens; ripples of light on the inner
curve of a bridge; a thing quite impossible to
capture.

He married, but, though he loved Elisabeth
after a manner, she failed to give him the thrill

15

for which he had grown weary with longing. She was the daughter of a well-known theatrical manager, a willowy, wispy, fair-haired girl with colorless eyes and pathetic little pimples just above that kind of small nose which English lady novelists call "retroussée" (note the second "e" added for safety). Her skin was so delicate that the least touch left a pink spot on it, slow to fade.

He married her because it just happened so. A trip to the mountains in her company, plus her fat brother and a remarkably athletic female cousin who, thank God, finally sprained an ankle in Pontresina, was chiefly responsible for their union. There was something so dainty, so airy about Elisabeth, and she had such a good-natured laugh. They were married in Munich in order to escape the onslaught of their many Berlin acquaintances. The chestnuts were in full bloom. A much treasured cigarette case was lost in a forgotten garden. One of the waiters at the hotel could speak seven languages. Elisabeth proved to have a tender little scar—the result of appendicitis.

She was a clinging little soul, docile and gentle. Her love was of the lily variety; but now and then it burst into flame and at such times Albinus was deluded into thinking that he had no need of any other love-mate.

16

When she became pregnant her eyes took on a vacant expression of contentment, as if she were contemplating that new inner world of hers; her careless walk changed to a careful waddle and she would greedily devour handfuls of snow which she hurriedly scooped up when no one was looking. Albinus did his best to look after her; took her out on long slow strolls; saw that she went to bed early and that household things with awkward corners were gentle to her when she moved about; but at night he dreamed of coming across a young girl lying asprawl on a hot lonely beach and in that dream a sudden fear would seize him of being caught by his wife. In the morning Elisabeth considered her swollen body in the wardrobe mirror and smiled a satisfied and mysterious smile. Then one day she was taken to a nursing home and Albinus lived for three weeks alone. He did not know what to do with himself; took a good deal of brandy; was tortured by two dark thoughts, each of a different kind of darkness: one was that his wife might die, and the other that if only he had a little more pluck he might find a friendly girl and bring her back to his empty bedroom.

Would the child ever be born? Albinus walked up and down the long, whitewashed, white-enameled passage with that nightmare palm in a pot at the top of the stairs; he hated it, hated the hopeless whiteness of the place and the ruddy-cheeked rustling hospital nurses with white-winged heads who kept trying to drive him away. At length the assistant surgeon emerged and said gloomily: "Well, it's all over." Before Albinus' eyes there appeared a fine dark rain like the flickering of some very old film (1910, a brisk jerky funeral procession with legs moving too fast). He rushed into the sickroom. Elisabeth had been happily delivered of a daughter.

The baby was at first red and wrinkled like a toy balloon on its decline. Soon, however, her face smoothed out and after a year she began to speak. Now, at the age of eight, she was far less voluble, for she had inherited her mother's reserved nature. Her gaiety, too, was like her mother's—a singular unobtrusive gaiety. It was just a quiet delight in one's own existence with a faint note of humorous surprise at being alive at all—yes, that was the tenor of it: mortal gaiety.

And throughout all these years Albinus remained faithful, with the duality of his feelings puzzling him a good deal. He felt that he loved his wife sincerely, tenderly—as much in fact as he was capable of loving a human being; and he was perfectly frank with her in everything except that secret foolish craving, that dream, that lust burning a hole in his life. She read all the letters which he wrote or received, liked to know the details of his business—especially those connected with the handling of old somber pictures, amid the cracks of which could be detected the white croup of a horse or a dusky smile. They had some very delightful trips abroad, and many beautifully soft evenings at home when he sat with her on the balcony high above the blue streets with the wires and chimneys drawn in Indian ink across the sunset, and reflected that he was really happy beyond his deserts.

One evening (a week before the talk about Axel Rex) he noticed on the way to a café where he had a business appointment that his watch was running amok (it was not the first time either) and that he had a full hour, a free gift to be used in some way. It was of course absurd to go back home to the other end of the town, yet neither did he feel disposed to sit and wait: the sight of other men with girl friends always upset him. He strolled about aimlessly and came to a small cinema the lights of which shed a scarlet sheen over the snow. He glanced at the poster (which portrayed a man looking up at a

window framing a child in a nightshirt), hesitated—and bought a ticket.

Hardly had he entered the velvety darkness
when the oval beam of an electric torch glided
toward him (as usually happens) and no less
swiftly and smoothly led him down the dark and
gently sloping gangway. Just as the light fell
on the ticket in his hand, Albinus saw the girl's
inclined face and then, as he walked behind her,
he dimly distinguished her very slight figure and
the even swiftness of her dispassionate movements. Whilst shuffling into his seat he looked
up at her and saw again the limpid gleam of her
eye as it chanced to catch the light and the melting outline of a cheek which looked as though
it were painted by a great artist against a rich
dark background. There was nothing very much
out of the common about all this: such things
had happened to him before and he knew that
it was unwise to dwell upon it. She moved away
and was lost in the darkness and he suddenly
felt bored and sad. He had come in at the end of
a film: a girl was receding among tumbled furniture before a masked man with a gun. There
was no interest whatever in watching happen-
ings which he could not understand since he had
not yet seen their beginning.

In the pause as soon as the lights were turned

on he noticed her again: she was standing at the exit next to a horribly purple curtain which she had just drawn to one side, and the outgoing people were surging past her. She was holding one hand in the pocket of her short embroidered apron and her black frock fitted her very tightly about the arms and bosom. He stared at her face almost in dread. It was a pale, sulky, painfully beautiful face. He guessed her age to be about eighteen.

Then, when the place had almost emptied and fresh people began to shuffle sideways along the rows, she passed to and fro, quite near to him several times; but he turned away because it hurt to look and because he could not help remembering how many times beauty—or what he called beauty—had passed him by and vanished.

For another half hour he sat in the darkness, his prominent eyes fixed on the screen. Then he rose and walked away. She drew the curtain aside for him with a slight clatter of wooden rings.

"Oh, but I will have one more look," thought Albinus miserably.

It seemed to him that her lips twitched a little. She let the curtain fall.

Albinus stepped into a blood-red puddle; the

snow was melting, the night was damp, with the fast colors of street lights all running and dissolving. "Argus"—good name for a cinema.

After three days he could ignore the memory of her no longer. He felt ridiculously excited as he entered the place once more—again in the middle of something. All was exactly as it had been the first time: the gliding torch, the long Luini-esque eyes, the swift walk in the darkness, the pretty movement of her black-sleeved arm as she clicked the curtain to one side. "Any normal man would know what to do," thought Albinus. A car was spinning down a smooth road with hairpin turns between cliff and abyss.

As he left, he tried to catch her eye, but failed. There was a steady downpour outside and the pavement glowed crimson.

Had he not gone there that second time he might perhaps have been able to forget this ghost of an adventure, but now it was too late. He went there a third time firmly resolved to smile at her—and what a desperate leer it would have been, had he achieved it. As it was, his heart thumped so that he missed his chance.

And the next day Paul came to dinner, they discussed the Rex affair, little Irma gobbled up her chocolate cream and Elisabeth asked her usual questions.

22

"Just dropped from the moon?" he asked, and then tried to make up for his nastiness by a belated titter.

After dinner he sat by his wife's side on the broad sofa, pecked at her with little kisses while she looked at gowns and things in a women's magazine, and dully he thought to himself:

"Damn it all, I'm happy, what more do I need? That creature gliding about in the dark. . . . Like to crush her beautiful throat. Well, she is dead anyway, since I shan't go there any more."

❧ 3 ❧

kill SHE was called Margot Peters. Her father was
a house-porter who had been badly shellshocked
in the War: his gray head jerked unceasingly
as if in constant confirmation of grievance and
woe, and he fell into a violent passion on the
slightest provocation. Her mother was still
youngish, but rather battered too—a coarse cal-
lous woman whose red palm was a perfect cor-
nucopia of blows. Her head was generally tied
up in a kerchief to keep the dust from her hair
during work, but after her great Saturday
clean-up—which was mainly effected by means
of a vacuum cleaner ingeniously connected to
the lift—she dressed herself up and sallied forth
to pay visits. She was unpopular with the tenants
on account of her insolence and the vicious way
she had of ordering people to wipe their feet on
the mat. The Staircase was the main idol of her
existence—not as a symbol of glorious ascension,

but as a thing to be kept nicely polished, so that her worst nightmare (after too generous a helping of potatoes and sauerkraut) was a flight of white steps with the black trace of a boot first right, then left, then right again and so on—up to the top landing. A poor woman indeed, and no object for derision.

Otto, Margot's brother, was three years her senior. He worked in a bicycle factory, despised his father's tame republicanism, held forth on politics in the neighboring pub and declared as he banged his fist on the table: "The first thing a man must have is a full belly." This was his guiding principle—and quite a sound one too.

As a child Margot went to school, and there she had her ears boxed rather less frequently than at home. A kitten's commonest movement is a soft little jump coming in sudden series; hers was a sharp raising of her left elbow to protect her face. In spite of all, she grew up into a bright and high-spirited girl. When only eight she joined with much gusto in the screaming, scraping games of football which schoolboys played in the middle of the street using a rubber ball the size of an orange. At ten she learned to ride her brother's bicycle. Bare-armed, with black pigtails flying, she scorched up and down the pavement; then halted with one foot resting on the curbstone, pensively. At twelve she became less boisterous. Those were the days when she liked nothing better than to stand at the door and chatter in undertones with the coalman's daughter, exchanging views upon the women who visited one of the lodgers, and discussing passing hats. Once she found on the staircase a shabby handbag containing a small cake of almond soap with a thin curved hair adhering to it, and half-a-dozen very queer photos. On another occasion the redhaired boy who always used to trip her up at play kissed her on the nape of the neck. Then one night she had a fit of hysterics, for which she got a dousing of cold water followed by a sound wallop.

A year later she had grown remarkably pretty, wore a short red frock and was mad on the movies. Afterward she remembered this period of her life with a strange oppressive feeling— the light, warm, peaceful evenings; the sound of the shops being bolted for the night; her father sitting astride on his chair outside the door, smoking his pipe and jerking his head; her mother, arms akimbo; the lilac bush leaning over the railing, Frau von Brock going home with her purchases in a green string-bag; Martha the maid waiting to cross with the greyhound and two wire-haired terriers. . . . It grew darker.

26

Her brother would come along with a couple of burly comrades who gathered round and jostled against her, plucking at her bare arms. One of them had eyes like the film actor Veidt. The street, with the upper stories of the houses still bathed in yellow light, grew quite silent. Only, across the way, two baldheaded men were playing cards on a balcony, and every guffaw and thump was audible.

When she was barely sixteen she became friendly with the girl who served behind the counter of a small stationery shop at the corner. This girl's young sister was already earning a decent living as an artist's model. So Margot dreamed of becoming a model, and then a film star. This transition seemed to her quite a simple matter: the sky was there, ready for her star. At about the same time she learned to dance, and now and then went with the shopgirl to the "Paradise" dance hall where elderly men made her extremely frank proposals to the crash and whine of a jazz band.

One day, as she was standing at the corner of the street, a fellow on a red motorcycle, whom she had observed once or twice already, drew up suddenly and offered her a ride. He had flaxen hair combed back and his shirt billowed behind, still full of the wind he had gathered.

She smiled, got up behind him, arranged her skirt and next moment was traveling at a terrific speed with his tie flying in her face. He took her outside the city and there halted. It was a sunny evening and a little party of midges were continuously darning the air in one spot. It was all very quiet: the quietude of pine and heather. He alighted and as he sat by her side at the edge of a ditch he told her that last year he had pushed on to Spain, just like this. Then he put his arm round her and began to squeeze and fumble and kiss her so violently that the discomfort she felt that day turned to dizziness. She wriggled free and began to cry. "You may kiss me," she sobbed, "but not that way, please." The youth shrugged his shoulders, started his engine, ran, jumped, swerved and was gone; leaving her sitting on a milestone. She returned home on foot. Otto, who had seen her go off, thumped his fist down on her neck and then kicked her skilfully, so that she fell and bruised herself against the sewing machine.

Next winter the shopgirl's sister introduced her to Frau Levandovsky, an elderly woman of goodly proportions with a genteel manner, albeit marred by a certain fruitiness of speech, and a large purple blotch on her cheek the size of a hand: she used to explain it by her mother's

28

having been frightened by a fire whilst expecting
her. Margot moved to a small servant's room in
her flat, and her parents were thankful to be rid
of her, the more so as they considered that any
job was sanctified by the money it brought in;
and fortunately her brother, who liked to speak
in threatening terms of capitalists' buying the
daughters of the poor, was away for a time, working at Breslau.

First Margot posed in the classroom of a
girls' school; then, later on, in a real studio where
she was drawn not only by women, but by men
also, most of whom were quite young. With her
sleek black hair nicely cut, she sat on a small
rug, stark naked, her feet curled under her, leaning on her blue-veined arm, her slim back (with
a sheen of fine down between the pretty shoulders, one of which was raised to her flaming
cheek) bent slightly forward in a semblance of
wistful weariness; she watched askance the students lift and lower their eyes and heard the
faint whir and grating of carbon pencils shad-
ing this curve or that. Out of sheer boredom she
used to pick out the best-looking man and throw
him a dark liquid glance whenever he raised his
face with its parted lips and puckered forehead.
She never succeeded in changing the color of his
attention, and this vexed her. Before, when she

had pictured herself sitting thus, alone in a pool of light, exposed to so many eyes, she had fancied that it would be rather exhilarating. But it made her stiff, that was all. To amuse herself she made up her face for the sitting, painted her dry hot mouth, darkened her eyelids, although indeed they were quite dark enough, and once even touched up her nipples with her lipstick. For this she got a good scolding from the Levandovsky woman.

So the days passed and Margot had only a very vague idea of what she was really aiming at, though there was always that vision of herself as a screen beauty in gorgeous furs being helped out of a gorgeous car by a gorgeous hotel porter under a giant umbrella. She was still wondering how to hop into that diamond bright world straight from the faded rug in the studio, when Frau Levandovsky told her for the first time about a lovesick young man from the provinces.

"You can't do without a boy friend," declared that lady complacently as she drank her coffee. "You are much too lively a lass not to need a companion, and this modest young fellow is wanting to find a pure soul in this wicked city."

Margot was holding Frau Levandovsky's fat yellow dachshund in her lap. She pulled up the animal's soft silky ears so as to make their tips meet over the gentle head (inside they resembled dark pink blotting paper, much used) and answered without looking up:

"Oh, there's no need for that yet. I'm only sixteen, aren't I? And what's the use? Does it lead you anywhere? I know those fellows."

"You're a fool," said Frau Levandovsky calmly. "I'm not talking to you about some scamp, but about a generous gentleman who saw you in the street and has been dreaming of you ever since."

"Some old dodderer, I expect," said Margot, kissing the wart on the dog's cheek.

"Fool," repeated Frau Levandovsky. "He is thirty, clean-shaven, distinguished, with a silk tie and a gold cigarette holder."

"Come, come for a walk," said Margot to the dog, and the dachshund slipped from her lap to the floor with a plop and trotted off along the passage.

Now the gentleman referred to by Frau Levandovsky was anything but a shy young man from the country. He had got in touch with her through two hearty commercial travelers with whom he had played poker on the boat train all the way from Bremen to Berlin. At first, nothing had been said about prices: the procuress had merely showed him a snapshot of a smiling girl with the sun in her eyes and a dog in her arms, and Miller (that was the name he gave) merely nodded. On the appointed day she bought some cakes and made plenty of coffee. Very shrewdly, she advised Margot to wear her old red frock. Toward six o'clock the bell rang.

"I'm not going to run any risks, I'm not," thought Margot. "If I hate him, I'll tell her so straight out, and if I don't I'll take my time to think it over."

Unfortunately it was not such a simple matter to decide what to make of Miller. First of all, he had a striking face. His lusterless black hair, carelessly brushed back, longish and with an odd dry look about it, was certainly not a wig, although it looked uncommonly like one. His cheeks seemed hollow because the cheekbones protruded so, and their skin was dull white as if coated with a thin layer of powder. His sharp twinkling eyes and those funny three-cornered nostrils which made one think of a lynx were never still for a moment; not so the heavy lower half of his face with the two motionless furrows at the corners of the mouth. His attire seemed rather foreign: that very blue shirt with a bright blue tie, that dark blue suit with enormously wide trousers. He was tall and slim and his square shoulders moved splendidly as he picked his way among Frau Levandovsky's plush furniture. Margot had pictured him quite differently and now she sat there with arms tightly crossed, feeling *Wow!* rather shocked and unhappy, while Miller fairly gobbled her up with his eyes. In a rasping voice he asked for her name. She told him.

"And I'm little Axel," he said with a short laugh, and brusquely turning away from her he resumed his conversation with Frau Levandovsky: they were talking sedately of Berlin sights and he was mockingly polite with his hostess.

Then suddenly he lapsed into silence, lit a cigarette and, picking off a bit of the cigarette paper which had stuck to his full, very red lip (where was the golden holder?), said:

"An idea, dear lady. Here's a stall for that Wagner thing; you're certain to like it. So put on your bonnet and toddle off. Take a taxi, I'll pay for that too."

Frau Levandovsky thanked him, but replied with some dignity that she preferred to remain at home.

"May I have a word with you?" asked Miller, obviously annoyed, rising from his chair.

"Have some more coffee," suggested the lady coolly.

33

Miller licked his chops and sat down again. Then he smiled, and in a new good-natured manner launched into a funny story about some friend of his, an opera singer who once, in the part of Lohengrin, being tight, failed to board the swan in time and waited hopefully for the next one. Margot bit her lips and then suddenly bent forward and went off into the most girlish fits of laughter. Frau Levandovsky laughed too, her large bosom quivering softly.

"Good," thought Miller, "if the old bitch wants me to play the lovesick fool, I shall—with a vengeance. I'll do it far more thoroughly and successfully than she supposes."

So he came next day, and then again and again. Frau Levandovsky, who had received only a small advance payment and wanted the whole sum, did not leave the pair alone for a moment. But sometimes when Margot took the dog for a walk late in the evening, Miller would suddenly emerge from the darkness and stroll along by her side. It flurried her so that she involuntarily hurried her steps, neglecting the dog, which followed with its body at a slight angle to the line of its wobbly trot. Frau Levandovsky got wind of these secret meetings and henceforth took out the dachshund herself.

More than a week passed in this manner. Then

Miller resolved to act. It would have been absurd
to pay the huge price demanded since he was on
the point of getting what he wanted without the
woman's help. One night he told her and Margot
three more funny stories, the funniest they had
yet heard, drank three cups of coffee and then,
walking up to Frau Levandovsky, gathered her
up in his arms, rushed her into the lavatory,
nimbly drew out the key, and locked the door
from the outside. The poor woman was so utterly taken aback at first that for five seconds at
least she did not utter a sound, but then—oh,
God! . . .

"Pack up your things quick and come along,"
said he, turning to Margot who was standing in
the middle of the room with both hands pressed
to her head.

He took her to a little flat which he had rented
for her the day before, and no sooner had Margot
crossed the threshold than she yielded with
pleasure and zest to the fate which had been lying in wait for her quite long enough.

And she liked Miller enormously. There was
something so satisfying about the grip of his
hands, the touch of his thick lips. He did not
speak to her much, but he often held her on his
knees and laughed quietly as he mused over
something unknown. She could not guess what

he was doing in Berlin or who he really was. Nor could she find out his hotel; and when she once tried searching his pockets, he gave her such a rap on the knuckles that she decided to do it better next time, but he was much too careful. Whenever he went out she was afraid that he would never come back; otherwise she was extraordinarily happy and hoped they would always be together. Now and then he gave her something—silk stockings, a powder puff—nothing very expensive. But he would take her to good restaurants and to the pictures and to a café afterward, and once, when she gasped as a famous film actor sat down a couple of tables away from them, he looked up at the man and they exchanged greetings, which made her gasp all the more sweetly.

He, for his part, developed such a taste for Margot that often, when he was on the point of going, he would suddenly shove his hat into a corner (incidentally, she had discovered from its inside that he had been to New York) and decided to stay. All this lasted for exactly one month. Then one morning he got up earlier than he usually did and said that he had to leave. She asked him for how long. He stared at her and then walked up and down the room in his purple pyjamas, rubbing his hands as though he were washing them.

"Forever, I guess," he said suddenly, and he began to dress without looking at her. She thought that he might be joking, kicked off the bedclothes, as the room was very hot, and turned her face to the wall.

"Pity I haven't a photo of you," he said as he stamped into his shoes.

Then she heard him pack and lock the small suitcase he used for the odds and ends he brought to the flat. After a few minutes he said:

"Don't move and don't look round."

She did not stir. What was he doing? She twitched her bare shoulder.

"Don't move," he repeated.

For a couple of minutes there was silence except for a faint grating sound which somehow seemed familiar.

"Now you may turn," he said.

But Margot still lay motionless. He walked up to her, kissed her ear and went out quickly. The kiss sang in her ear for quite a while.

She lay in bed the whole day. He never came back.

Next morning she received a wire from Bremen: "Rooms paid till July adieu sweet devil."

37

"Good Heavens, how shall I do without him?" said Margot aloud. She leaped to the window, flung it open and was about to throw herself out. But at that moment a red-and-gold fire engine drove up, snorting loudly, and stopped in front of the house opposite. A crowd had collected, clouds of smoke billowed from the top window, and black scraps of charred paper floated in the wind. She was so interested in the fire that she forgot her intention.

She had very little money left. In her distress she went to a dance hall as abandoned damsels do in films. Two Japanese gentlemen accosted her and, as she had taken more cocktails than were good for her, she agreed to spend the night with them. Next morning she demanded two hundred marks. The Japanese gentlemen gave her three fifty in small change and bustled her out. She resolved to be more wary in the future.

At a bar one night a fat old man with a nose like an overripe pear put his wrinkled hand on her silken knee and said wistfully:

"Glad to meet you again, Dora. Do you still remember what fun we had last summer?"

She laughed and replied that he had made a mistake. The old man asked her with a sigh what she would drink. Then he drove her home and became so beastly in the darkness of the car that she jumped out. He followed her and almost in tears begged her to meet him again. She gave him her telephone number. When he had paid for her room till November and had also given her enough money to buy a fur coat, she allowed him to stay for the night. He was a comfortable bedfellow, dropping fast asleep the moment he had stopped wheezing. Then he failed to keep an appointment, and when at last she rang up his office she was told that he was dead.

She sold her fur coat and the money kept her until the spring. Two days before this transaction she felt an ardent longing to display herself to her parents in her splendor, so she drove past the house in a taxicab. It was a Saturday and her mother was polishing the handle of the front door. When she saw her daughter, she stopped dead. "Well, I never!" she exclaimed with much feeling. Margot smiled silently, got back into the cab and through the back window saw her brother come running out of the house. He bawled something after her and shook his fist.

She took a cheaper room. Half undressed, her little feet shoeless, she would sit on the edge of her bed in the gathering darkness and smoke endless cigarettes. Her landlady, a sympathetic body, dropped in now and then for a soulful chat and one day told Margot that a cousin of hers owned a little cinema which was doing quite well. The winter seemed colder than winters used to be; Margot looked about her for something to pawn: that sunset perhaps.

"What shall I do next?" she thought.

One raw blue morning when her courage was high she made up her face very strikingly, looked up a film company with a promising name and succeeded in making an appointment to see the manager at his office. He turned out to be an elderly man with a black bandage over his right eye and a piercing gleam in his left. Margot began assuring him that she had played before—and very successfully.

"What picture?" asked the manager gazing benevolently at her excited face.

Boldly she mentioned a firm, a film. The man was silent. Then he closed his left eye (it would have been a wink, had the other been visible) and said:

"Lucky for you that you came across me. Another in my place might have been tempted by your . . . er . . . youth to make you heaps of fine promises and—well, you'd have gone the way of all flesh, never to become the silver ghost of romance—at least of that special brand of romance which we deal in. I am, as you may observe, no longer young, and what I haven't seen of life isn't worth seeing. My daughter, I imagine, is older than you. And for that reason I would like to tell you something, my dear child. You have never been an actress and in all likelihood you never will be. Go home, think it over, talk to your parents if you are on speaking terms with them, which I doubt . . ."

Margot slapped the edge of the desk with her glove, stood up and stalked out, her face distorted with fury.

Another company had its office in the same building, but there she was not even admitted. Full of wrath she made her way home. Her landlady boiled her two eggs and patted her shoulders, while Margot ate greedily, angrily. Then the good woman fetched some brandy and two small glasses, filled them with a shaky hand, carefully corked the bottle and carried it away.

"Here's to your good luck," she said, seating herself again at the rickety table. "Everything'll be all right, my dear. I'll be seeing my cousin tomorrow and we'll have a chat about you."

The chat was quite a success, and at first Margot enjoyed her new occupation, though it was, of course, a little humiliating to start her film career in *that* way. Three days later she felt as though she had done nothing else all her life but show groping people to their seats. On Fri-

41

day, however, there was a change of program
and that cheered her up. She stood in the darkness leaning against the wall and watched Greta
Garbo. But after a while she was fed up for good.
Another week went by. A man coming out lingered by the exit and glanced at her with a shy
helpless expression. After two or three nights he
returned. He was perfectly dressed and his blue
eyes stared at her hungrily.

"Quite a decent-looking fellow, though rather
on the dull side," mused Margot.

Then, when he turned up for the fourth or
fifth time—and certainly not for the sake of the
picture, because it was the same—she felt a faint
thrill of pleasant excitement.

But how timid he was, that fellow! As she was
leaving for home one night, she noticed him on
the other side of the street. She walked slowly
on without looking round, but with the corners of
her eyes folded back like the ears of a rabbit:
expecting that he would follow her. But he did
not—he simply faded away. Then, when he came
again to the "Argus" there was a wan, morbid,
very interesting look about him. Her work over,
Margot tripped out into the street; stopped;
opened her umbrella. There he was standing
again on the opposite sidewalk and calmly she

42

crossed over to him. But when he saw her approaching, he at once began to walk away.

He felt silly and sick. He knew that she was behind and so was afraid to walk too fast lest he should lose her; but then, too, he was afraid to slacken his pace lest she should overtake him. At the next street-crossing he was obliged to wait while car after car sped past him. Here she overtook him, all but slipped under a bicycle van and jumped back, colliding with him. He grasped her thin elbow and they crossed together.

"Now it has started," thought Albinus, awkwardly adjusting his stride to hers—he had never walked with so small a woman.

"You're drenched," she said with a smile. He took the umbrella out of her hand; she pressed still closer to him. For a moment he feared that his heart might burst, but then suddenly something relaxed delightfully as though he had caught the tune of his ecstasy, this moist ecstasy drumming, drumming against the taut silk overhead. Now his words came freely and he enjoyed their newborn ease.

The rain stopped, but they still walked under the umbrella. When they came to a halt at her front door, he closed the wet, shiny, beautiful thing and gave it back to her.

"Don't go away yet," he pleaded (holding the while one hand in his pocket and endeavoring to push off his wedding ring with his thumb). "Don't," he repeated (it came off).

"Getting late," she said, "my aunt will be angry."

He seized her by the wrists and with the violence of shyness tried to kiss her, but she ducked and his lips met only her velvet cap.

"Let me go," she murmured, her head lowered. "You know you ought not to do that."

"But don't go," he cried. "I have no one in the world but you."

"I can't, I can't," she answered, and turning the key in the lock she pressed against the great door with her small shoulder.

"I shall wait for you again tomorrow," said Albinus.

She smiled at him through the glass pane and then ran down the dim passage toward the back yard.

He took a deep breath, groped for his handkerchief, blew his nose, carefully buttoned, then unbuttoned, his overcoat, noticed how light and bare his hand felt and hurriedly slipped on the ring, which was still quite warm.

৶ 4 ৸

At home nothing had changed, and this seemed remarkable. Elisabeth, Irma, Paul, belonged, as it were, to another period, limpid and tranquil like the backgrounds of the early Italians. Paul, after working all day at his office, liked to pass a quiet evening at his sister's home. He cherished a profound respect for Albinus, for his learning and taste, for the beautiful things around him—for the spinach-green Gobelin in the dining room, a hunt in a forest.

When Albinus opened the door of his flat he felt a queer sinking in the pit of his stomach as he reflected that, in a moment, he would see his wife: would she not be able to read his perfidy in his face? For that walk in the rain was betrayal; all that had gone before had been only thoughts and dreams. Perhaps, by some dreadful mischance, his actions had been observed and reported? Perhaps he smelt of the cheap sweet scent she used? As he stepped into the hall he swiftly concocted in his mind a story that might come in handy: of a young artist, her poverty and her talent, and how he was trying to help her. But nothing had changed, neither the white door behind which his daughter was sleeping at the end of the passage, nor his brother-in-law's vast overcoat which was hanging on its coat-hanger (a special hanger wound in red silk) as calmly and respectably as ever.

He entered the sitting room. Here they were—Elisabeth in her familiar tweed dress with checks, Paul puffing at his cigar, and an old lady of their acquaintance, a baron's widow who had been impoverished by the inflation and now carried on a small business in rugs and pictures. . . . No matter what they were discussing: the rhythm of everyday life was so comforting that he felt a spasm of joy: he had not been found out.

And then later as he lay by his wife's side in their bedroom, dimly lit, quietly furnished, with, as usual, part of the central heating apparatus (painted white) reflected in the mirror, Albinus marveled at his own divided nature: his affection for Elisabeth was perfectly secure and undiminished, but at the same time there burned in his mind the thought that perhaps no later than tomorrow—yes, certainly tomorrow—

46

But it did not prove quite so easy. At their next meetings Margot skilfully contrived to avoid his love-making—and there was not the slightest chance of his being able to take her to a hotel. She did not tell him much about herself—only that she was an orphan, the daughter of a painter (curious coincidence, that), and lived with her aunt; that she was very hard up, but longed to give up her exhausting job.

Albinus had introduced himself to her under the hurriedly assumed name of Schiffermiller, and Margot thought bitterly: "Another Miller—already," and then: "Oh, you're lying, of course."

March was rainy. These nocturnal strolls under the umbrella tortured Albinus, so he soon suggested they should go into a café. He selected a dingy little place where he felt sure of not meeting any acquaintances.

It was his habit when settling down at a table to lay out at once his cigarette case and lighter. On the case Margot espied his initials. She said nothing, but after a little reflection asked him to fetch her the telephone book. While he was walking toward the booth with his slow flopping gait, she took up his hat from the chair and swiftly examined its lining: there was his name (he had had it put there in order to thwart absent-minded artists at parties).

Presently he came back with the telephone directory, holding it like a Bible, smiling tenderly, and, while he was gazing at her long drooping lashes, Margot sped through the R's and found Albinus' address and his telephone number. Then she quietly closed the well-thumbed blue volume.

"Take off your coat," murmured Albinus.

Without bothering to stand up she began to wriggle out of the sleeves, inclining her pretty neck and thrusting forward first the right and then the left shoulder. As Albinus helped her, he caught a hot whiff of violets and saw her shoulder blades move, and the sallow skin between them ripple and smooth out again. Then she took off her hat, peered into her pocket-mirror and, wetting her forefinger, tapped the black lovelocks on her temples.

Albinus sat down beside her and looked and looked at that face in which everything was so charming—the burning cheeks, the lips glistening from the cherry brandy, the childish solemnity of the long hazel eyes and the small downy mole on the soft curve just beneath the left one.

"If I knew I should hang for it," he thought, "I would still look at her."

Even that vulgar Berlin slang of hers only enhanced the charm of her throaty voice and large

48

white teeth. When laughing she half closed her eyes and a dimple danced on her cheek. He pawed at her little hand, but she withdrew it briskly.

"You're driving me crazy," he said.

Margot patted his cuff and said:

"Now, be a good boy."

His first thought next morning was: it can't go on like this, it just can't. I must get her a room. Curse that aunt. We shall be alone, quite alone. A textbook of love for beginners. Oh, the things I shall teach her. So young, so pure, so maddening . . .

"Are you asleep?" asked Elisabeth softly.

He achieved the perfect yawn and opened his eyes. Elisabeth was seated in her pale blue nightgown on the edge of the double bed and was looking through the mail.

"Anything interesting?" asked Albinus, gazing in dull wonder at her white shoulder.

"Ach, he asks you for money again. Says his wife and his mother-in-law have been ill and that people are plotting against him. Says he can't afford to buy paints. We'll have to help him again, I suppose."

"Yes, of course," said Albinus, and in his mind there formed an extraordinary, vivid picture of Margot's dead father: he, too, no doubt had been a seedy, bad-tempered and not very gifted artist whom life had treated harshly.

"And here's an invitation to the Artists' Club. We shall have to go this time. And here's a letter from the States."

"Read it aloud," he asked.

"My dear Sir, I am afraid I have not much news to convey, but still there are a few things I should like to add to my last long letter, which, in parenthesis, you have not answered yet. As I may be coming in the Fall . . ."

At that moment the telephone rang on the bed-side table. "Tut, tut," said Elisabeth, and leaned forward. Albinus followed absent-mindedly the movements of her delicate fingers as they took and clasped the white receiver, and then he heard the tiny ghost of a voice squeaking at the other end.

"Oh, good morning," exclaimed Elisabeth, at the same time making a certain face at her husband, a sure sign that it was the Baroness talking, and talking a lot.

He stretched out his hand for the American letter and glanced at the date. Funny he had not yet answered the last one. Irma came in to greet her parents as she did every morning. Silently she kissed her father and then her mother, who was listening to the telephone tale with closed eyes,

50

grunting every now and then in misplaced assent or feigned astonishment.

"See that you are a very good little girl today," whispered Albinus to his daughter. With a smile Irma disclosed a fistful of marbles.

She was not at all pretty; freckles covered her pale bumpy forehead, her eyelashes were much too fair, her nose too long for her face.

"By all means," said Elisabeth, and sighed with relief as she hung up.

Albinus prepared to go on with the letter. Elisabeth held her daughter by the wrists and was telling her something funny, laughing, kissing her and giving her a little tug after every sentence. Irma went on smiling demurely, as she shuffled with her shoe on the floor. Again the telephone rang. This time Albinus attended to it.

"Good morning, Albert dear," said a feminine voice.

"Who—" began Albinus, and suddenly he had the sickening sensation of going down a very fast lift.

"It was not particularly nice of you to give me a false name," pursued the voice, "but I forgive you. I just wanted to tell you—"

"Wrong number," said Albinus hoarsely, and crashed back the receiver. At the same time he reflected with dismay that Elisabeth might have

51

heard something just as he had heard the Baroness' minute voice.

"What was it?" she asked. "Why have you
turned so red?"

"Absurd! Irma, my child, run along, don't
fidget about like that. Utterly absurd. That's the
tenth wrong call in two days. He writes that he'll
probably be coming here at the end of the year.
I'll be glad to see him."

"Who writes?"

"Good God! You never get what one's saying.
That man from America. That fellow Rex."

"What Rex?" asked Elisabeth unconcernedly.

❧ 5 ❧

THEIR meeting that night was a tempestuous one. Albinus had stayed at home all day because he was in a panic that she might ring up again. When she emerged from the "Argus" he greeted her incontinently with:

"Look here, child, I forbid you to ring me up. It won't do. If I did not give you my name, I had my reasons for it."

"Oh, that's all right. I'm through with you," said Margot blandly, and walked away.

He stood there and stared after her helplessly.

What an ass he was! He ought to have held his tongue; then she'd have fancied she had made a mistake, after all. Albinus overtook her and walked along by her side.

"Forgive me," he said. "Don't be cross with me, Margot. I can't live without you. Look here, I've thought it all over. Drop your job. I'm rich.

You shall have your own room, your own flat, anything you like . . ."

"You're a liar, a coward and a fool," said Margot (summing him up rather neatly) . "And you're married—that's why you hide that ring in your mackintosh pocket. Oh, of course, you're married; else you wouldn't have been so rude on the 'phone."

"And if I am?" he asked. "Won't you meet me any more?"

"What does it matter to me? Deceive her; it'll do her good."

"Margot, stop," groaned Albinus.

"Leave me alone."

"Margot, listen to me. It is true, I have a family, but please, please, stop jeering about it . . . Oh, don't go away," he cried, catching her, missing her, clutching at her shabby little handbag.

"Go to hell!" she shouted, and banged the door in his face.

54

"I'D LIKE my fortune told," said Margot to her landlady, and the latter took out from behind the empty beer bottles a decrepit pack of cards most of which had lost their corners so that they looked almost circular. A rich man with dark hair, troubles, a feast, a long journey . . .

"I must find out how he lives," thought Margot, her elbows resting on the table. "Perhaps after all he is not really wealthy, and it's not worth my while to bother about him. Or shall I risk it?"

The next morning at exactly the same time she rang him up again. Elisabeth was in her bath. Albinus spoke almost in a whisper with his eye on the door. Although sick with fear, he was madly happy to be forgiven.

"My darling," he murmured, "my darling."

"Say, what time will wifey be away from home?" she asked laughing.

"I'm afraid I don't know," he answered with a cold shiver. "Why?"

"I'd like to drop in for a moment."

He was silent. Somewhere a door opened.

"I can't go on talking," murmured Albinus.

"If I come to you I might kiss you."

"Today, I don't know. No," he stammered, "I don't think it's feasible. If I suddenly ring off don't be surprised. I shall see you tonight, and then we'll . . ." He hung up and sat for some time motionless, listening to the pounding of his heart. "I suppose I *am* a coward," he thought. "She's sure to dawdle in the bathroom for another half hour."

"One small request," he said to Margot when they met. "Let's take a taxi."

"An open one," said Margot.

"No, that's too dangerous. I promise you I'll behave," he added as he gazed lovingly at her childishly upturned face which looked very white in the blaze of the street lamp.

"Listen," he began when they were seated in the cab. "First I am not angry with you, of course, for ringing me up, but I beg you, I implore you, not to do it again, my darling, my precious." ("That's better," thought Margot.)

"And secondly, tell me how you found out my name?"

She lied, quite needlessly, telling him that a woman she knew had seen them in the street together and knew him too.

"Who was it?" asked Albinus with horror.

"Oh, just a working woman. I think one of her sisters was once cook or housemaid in your family."

Albinus racked his memory despairingly.

"Anyway, I told her she was wrong. I'm a smart little girl."

The darkness inside the taxi slid and swayed as quarters and halves and whole squares of ashen light passed from window to window across it. Margot was sitting so near that he felt the blissful animal warmth of her body. "I shall die or go off my head if I can't have her," thought Albinus.

"And thirdly," he said aloud, "find yourself lodgings, say two or three rooms and a kitchen— that is, upon condition that you let me visit you occasionally."

"Albert, have you already forgotten what I suggested this morning?"

"But it's so risky," groaned Albinus. "You see . . . Tomorrow, for instance, I'll be alone from about four to six, but one never knows what may happen . . ." and he pictured to himself how his wife might come back for something she had forgotten.

"But I've told you I'd kiss you," said Margot softly, "and then, you know, there's not a thing in the world that can't be explained away somehow."

So next day, when Elisabeth and Irma had gone out for tea, he sent Frieda the maid (it was cook's day out, luckily) on a good long errand with a couple of books to deliver miles away.

Now he was alone. His watch had stopped some minutes ago, but the clock in the dining room was exact and then, too, by craning out of the window he could see the church clock. A quarter past four. It was a bright windy day in mid-April. On the sunlit wall of the opposite house the fast shadow of smoke ran sideways from the shadow of a chimney. The asphalt was drying patchily after a recent shower, the damp still showing in the form of grotesque black skeletons as if painted across the width of the road.

Half past four. She might come at any minute. Whenever he thought of Margot's slim girlish figure, her silky skin, the touch of her funny, ill-kept little hands, he felt a rush of desire which was almost painful. Now, the vision of the promised kiss filled him with such ecstasy that it seemed hardly possible it could be still further intensified. And yet beyond it, down a vista of mirrors, there was still to be reached the dim

58

white form of her body, that very form which art students had sketched so conscientiously and so badly. But of those dull hours in the studio Albinus suspected nothing, although, by a queer trick of fate, he had unwittingly seen her nude form already: the family doctor, old Lampert, had shown him some charcoal drawings which his son had made two years ago and among them was a girl with bobbed hair, her feet curled under her on the rug where she sat, leaning on her stiff arm, her shoulder touching her cheek. "No, I think I prefer the hunchback," he had remarked, turning back to another sheet on which a bearded cripple was depicted. "Yes, it is a great pity he has given up Art," he had added, closing the portfolio.

Ten minutes to five. She was already twenty minutes late. "I'll wait until five and then go out," he murmured.

Suddenly he saw her. She was crossing the street without coat or hat, as though she lived round the corner.

"Still time to run down and tell her it's getting too late now," but instead of doing so Albinus tiptoed breathlessly into the hall, and when he heard the childish stamping of her footsteps coming up the stairs he noiselessly opened the door.

Margot in her short red frock with bare arms smiled into the mirror and then twirled round on her heel, as she smoothed the back of her head.

"You do live in style," she said, her beaming eyes roaming over the hall with its large rich pictures, its porcelain vase in the corner and that cream-colored cretonne instead of _wallpaper. "This way?" she asked and pushed open a door. "Oh!" she said.

He laid one trembling hand round her waist and with her he looked up at the crystal chandelier as though he himself were a stranger. But he saw it all through a swimming haze. She crossed her feet and rocked gently as she stood there, her eyes roaming.

"You are rich," she said as they entered the next room. "Heavens, what rugs!"

She was so overcome by the sideboard in the dining room that Albinus was able to finger her ribs stealthily and, above them, a hot soft muscle.

"Let's go on," she said eagerly.

In a passing mirror he saw a pale grave gentleman walking beside a schoolgirl in her Sunday dress. Cautiously, he stroked her smooth arm and the glass grew dim.

"Come on," said Margot.

He wanted to get her back into the study. Then, if his wife came back earlier than he expected, it would be simple: a young artist in want of help.

"And what's in there?" she asked.

"That's the nursery. You've seen everything now."

"Let me go," she said, moving her shoulders.

He drew a deep breath.

"It's the nursery, my darling. Only the nursery —there's nothing to see."

But she went inside and suddenly he felt a strange impulse to shout at her: "Please, don't touch anything." But she was already holding a purple plush elephant. He snatched it away and shoved it into a corner. Margot laughed.

"Your little girl is in clover here," she said. Then she opened the next door.

"That's enough, Margot," Albinus pleaded, "we are getting too far from the hall, we shan't hear the front door. It's dreadfully dangerous."

But she shook him off like a naughty child and slipped through the passage into the bedroom. There she seated herself in front of the mirror (mirrors were having plenty of work that day), turned a silver-backed brush in her hand, sniffed at a silver-stopped bottle.

"Oh, don't!" cried Albinus.

She swerved by him neatly, ran to the double bed, and seated herself on the edge. She pulled up her stocking like a child, made the garter snap, and showed him the tip of her tongue.

". . . and then I'll kill myself," thought Albinus, suddenly losing his head.

He lurched toward her, his arms open, but she bounded past him with a chirrup of glee and bolted out of the room. He made a belated dash after her. Margot slammed the door and, panting and laughing, turned the key from outside. (Oh, how the poor fat woman had banged and thumped and yelled!)

"Margot, open at once," said Albinus softly.

He heard her footsteps dancing away.

"Open," he repeated in a louder voice.

Silence.

"The little vixen," he thought, "what an absurd situation!"

He was frightened. He was hot. He was not used to bouncing about rooms. He was in an agony of thwarted desire. Had she really gone? No, someone was walking about the flat. He tried some keys he had in his pocket; then, losing his temper, shook the door violently.

"Open at once. Do you hear?"

The footsteps drew near. It was not Margot.

"Hullo. What's the matter?" asked an unexpected voice—Paul's! "Are you locked in? Shall I let you out?"

The door opened. Paul looked alarmed. "What has happened, old man?" he repeated and gaped at the hairbrush lying on the floor.

"Oh, a ridiculous thing . . . Tell you in a moment . . . Let's have a glass of something."

"You gave me the devil of a shock," said Paul. "I could not think what on earth had happened. Lucky I came along. Elisabeth told me she'd be home about six. Lucky I was rather early. Who locked you in? Not your maid gone mad, I hope?"

Albinus stood with his back to him and busied himself with the brandy.

"Didn't you meet anybody on the stairs?" he asked, trying to speak distinctly.

"I took the lift," said Paul.

"Saved," thought Albinus, his spirits reviving considerably. (But how dangerously foolish to have forgotten that Paul, too, had a key to the flat!)

"Would you believe it," he said, as he sipped the brandy, "a burglar broke in. Don't tell Elisabeth, of course. Thought there was no one at home, I expect. Suddenly I heard the front door behaving oddly. I came out of my study to see what it was clicking—and there was a man slipping into the bedroom. I followed him and tried to grab him, but he sort of doubled back and locked

63

me in. It's a great pity he escaped. I thought you might have met him."

"You're joking," said Paul aghast.

"No, not at all. I was in my study and heard the front door clicking. So I went to see what it was and . . ."

"But he may have stolen something, let's look. And we must inform the police."

"Oh, he hadn't time," said Albinus, "it all happened in a second; I scared him away."

"What did he look like?"

"Oh, just a man with a cap. A largish man. Very strong-looking."

"He could have hurt you! What a very unpleasant experience. Come on, we must have a look round."

They went through the rooms. Examined locks. Everything was in order. It was only at the end of their investigations, as they were walking through the library, that suddenly a pang of horror shot through Albinus: there, in a corner between the shelves, just behind a revolving bookstand, the edge of a bright red frock was showing. By some miracle Paul did not see it, although he was nosing about conscientiously. There was a collection of miniatures in the next room and he pored over the inclined glass.

"That's enough, Paul," said Albinus huskily.

"There is no point in going on. It's quite clear he hasn't taken anything."

"How shaken you look," exclaimed Paul, as they returned to the study. "My poor chap! Look here, you must have your lock changed, or always keep the door bolted. And what about the police? Would you like me to—"

"Ssh," hissed Albinus.

Voices drew near and Elisabeth came in, followed by Irma, her nurse and one of her little friends—a fat child who, in spite of her shy stolid expression, could be most boisterous. Albinus felt as if it were all a nightmare. Margot's presence in the house was monstrous, unbearable . . . The maid returned—with the books—she had not found the address, and no wonder! The nightmare grew wilder. He suggested going to the theater that night, but Elisabeth said she was tired. At supper he was so busy straining his ears for any suspicious rustle that he did not notice what he was eating (cold beef, in fact, with pickles). Paul kept on looking round, giving out little coughs, or humming—if only, thought Albinus, the meddlesome fool would remain in his place and not potter about. But there was another dreadful possibility: the children might start romping through all the rooms; and he dared not go and lock the door of the library; that might lead to unimaginable complications. Thank God, Irma's little friend soon left, and Irma was popped to bed. But the tension remained. He felt as if they all— Elisabeth, Paul, the maid and himself—were sprawling over the whole place instead of keeping huddled together, as they should, in order to give Margot a chance of slipping out; if, indeed, she had that intention.

At length, at about eleven o'clock, Paul left. As usual, Frieda chained and bolted the door. Now Margot could not get out!

"I'm awfully sleepy," said Albinus to his wife and yawned nervously, and then could not stop yawning. They went to bed. In the house all was silent. Elisabeth was just about to turn out the light.

"You get to sleep," he said. "I think I'll go and read a bit."

She smiled drowsily, heedless of his inconsistency. "Don't wake me up when you come," she murmured.

Everything was too quiet to be natural. It seemed as if the silence was rising, rising—would suddenly brim over and break into laughter. He had slipped out of bed, and in his nightsuit and felt slippers was walking noiselessly down the passage. Strange: all dread had gone. The nightmare

66

had melted into the keen, sweet sensation of absolute freedom, peculiar to sinful dreams.

Albinus undid the neck of his pyjamas as he crept along. He was trembling all over. "In a moment—in a moment she will be mine," he thought. Softly he opened the door of the library and turned on the softly shaded light.

"Margot, you mad little thing," he whispered feverishly.

But it was only a scarlet silk cushion which he himself had brought there a few days ago, to crouch on while consulting Nonnenmacher's *History of Art*—ten volumes, folio.

⋘ 7 ⋙

MARGOT informed her landlady that she would soon be leaving. It was all going splendidly. In his flat she had realized the soundness of her admirer's wealth. Also, to judge by the photograph on his bed table, his wife was not at all as she had imagined her—a large stately woman with a grim expression and a grip of iron; on the contrary, she seemed a quiet, vague sort of creature who could be got out of the way without much trouble.

And she quite liked Albinus: he was a well-groomed gentleman smelling of talcum powder and good tobacco. Of course, she could not hope for a repetition of the ecstasy of her first love affair. And she would not let herself think of Miller, of his chalk-white hollow cheeks, unkempt black hair and long skilful hands.

Albinus could soothe her and allay her fever—like those cool plantain leaves which it is so com-

68

forting to apply to an inflamed spot. Then there was something else. He was not only well-to-do, but also belonged to a world which afforded easy access to the stage and the films. Often, behind her locked door, she would make all sorts of wonderful faces for the benefit of her dressing-chest mirror or recoil before the barrel of an imaginary revolver. And it seemed to her that she simpered and sneered as well as any screen actress.

After a thorough and painstaking search she found quite a pretty suite of rooms in a very good neighborhood. Albinus was so upset after her visit that she felt sorry for him and made no further difficulty about taking the fat wad of notes which he crammed into her bag during their evening walk. Moreover, she let him kiss her in the shelter of a porch. The fire of this kiss was still around him like a colored glory when he returned home. He could not lay it aside in the hall as he did his black felt hat, and when he came into the bedroom he thought that his wife must see that halo.

But it never even occurred to Elisabeth, placid, thirty-five-year-old Elisabeth, that her husband might deceive her. She knew that he had had little adventures before his marriage, and she remembered that she herself, as a small girl, had been secretly in love with an old actor who used to visit her father and enliven dinner with beautiful imitations of farmyard sounds. She had heard and read that husbands and wives constantly deceived one another; indeed, adultery was the core of gossip, romantic poetry, funny stories and famous operas. But she was quite simply and steadfastly convinced that her own marriage was a very special, precious and pure tie that could never be broken.

Her husband's evenings out, which, he explained, were spent with some artists interested in that cinema idea of his, never afforded her the least suspicion. His irritability and jumpiness she put down to the weather, which was quite unusual for May: at one moment it was hot, at the next there would be icy torrents of rain, mixed with hailstones that bounced on the window sills like tiny tennis balls.

"Shall we go for a trip somewhere?" she suggested casually one day. "Tyrol? Rome?"

"You go, if you want to," replied Albinus; "I have lots to do, my dear."

"Oh, no, it was just a fancy," she said, and set off with Irma to the Zoo to see the baby elephant, which turned out to have hardly any trunk at all and a fringe of short hair standing on end all along its back.

With Paul it was a different matter. The episode of the locked door had left him with a strange uneasiness. Albinus had not only failed to notify the police, but he was actually annoyed when Paul returned to the subject. So Paul could not help brooding over the thing. He tried to recall whether he *had*, perhaps, seen any suspicious character when he came into the house and walked toward the lift. He was very observant, he thought: he had, for instance, noticed a cat which sprang as he passed, and slithered between the bars of the garden railings, a schoolgirl in red for whom he had held open the door, broadcast laughter and song from the porter's lodge where the wireless was turned on as usual. Yes, the burglar must have run down while he was going up in the lift. But what gave him that nasty feeling?

His sister's married happiness was to him a sacred thing. When, some days later, he was put through on the telephone to Albinus, while the latter was still talking, and so overheard certain words (fate's classical method: eavesdropping), he almost swallowed a piece of matchwood with which he was picking his teeth.

"Don't ask me, just buy what you like."

"But don't you see, Albert . . ." said a vulgar, capricious feminine voice.

With a shudder Paul hung up the receiver as

though he had inadvertently caught hold of a snake.

That evening, as he sat with his sister and brother-in-law, he could not think of anything to talk about. He just sat there, self-conscious and fidgety, rubbing his chin, crossing and re-crossing his plump legs, looking at his watch and putting the blank handless thing back into his waistcoat pocket. He was one of those sensitive beings who blush guiltily when someone else makes a blunder.

Could this man whom he loved and revered be deceiving Elisabeth? "No, no, it's a mistake, some silly misunderstanding," he kept telling himself, as he glanced at Albinus who was reading a book with unruffled countenance, clearing his throat now and then, and very carefully cutting the pages with an ivory paper knife . . . "Impossible! That locked bedroom door put it into my mind. The words I heard doubtless admit of some innocent explanation. How could anyone deceive Elisabeth?"

She was cuddled in a corner of the sofa, relating slowly and minutely the plot of a play which she had seen. Her pale eyes with the faint freckles under them were as candid as her mother's had been, and her unpowdered nose shone pathetically. Paul nodded his head and smiled. She might have been speaking Russian for all he knew. Then suddenly, and for one second only, he caught sight of Albinus' eyes looking at him over the book he was holding.

◦§ 8 §◦

MEANWHILE Margot had rented the flat and
proceeded to buy a number of household articles,
beginning with a refrigerator. Although Albinus
paid up handsomely, and even with a certain
pleasurable emotion, he was giving the money on
trust, for not only had he not seen the flat—he
did not even know its address. She had told him
that it would be such fun if he did not see her
home until it was complete.

A week passed. He fancied that she would
ring him up on Saturday. The whole day he
mounted guard over the telephone. But it
gleamed and was mute. On Monday he decided
that she had tricked him—had vanished forever.
In the evening Paul came. These visits were hell
for both of them by now. Still worse—Elisabeth
was not at home. Paul sat in the study opposite
Albinus, and smoked, and looked at the tip of
his cigar. He had even become thinner of late.

74

"He knows everything," thought Albinus dismally. "Well, and what if he does? He's a man; he ought to understand."

Irma trotted in and Paul's countenance brightened. He took her on his lap and produced a funny little grunt as she prodded him with her small fist in the stomach while making herself comfortable.

Then Elisabeth returned from a bridge-tea. The thought of supper and of the long evening afterward suddenly seemed to Albinus more than he could endure. He announced that he was not supping at home; his wife asked him good-naturedly why he had not said so before.

He had only one wish: to find Margot immediately, no matter what the cost. Destiny, which had promised him so much, had not the right to cheat him now. He was so desperate that he resolved upon a very daring step. He knew where her old room was, and he knew that she had lived there with her aunt. Thither he went. As he walked through the back yard, he saw a servant-girl making a bed at an open window on the ground floor and questioned her.

"Fräulein Peters?" she repeated, holding the pillow she had been thumping. "Oh, I think she has moved. But you'd better see for yourself. Fifth floor, door on the left."

A slatternly woman with bloodshot eyes opened the door a little way without taking off the chain, and asked what he wanted.

"I want to know Fräulein Peters' new address. She used to live here with her aunt."

"Oh, did she?" said the woman with sudden interest; and now she unhooked the chain. She led him into a tiny parlor, all the objects in which shook and rattled at the least movement. On a piece of American cloth with brown circular stains stood a plate of mashed potatoes, salt in a torn paper bag and three empty beer bottles. With a mysterious smile she invited him to be seated.

"If I was her aunt," she said with a wink, "I'd not be likely to know her address. No," she added with a certain vehemence, "she hasn't got no aunt."

"Drunk," thought Albinus wearily. "Look here," he said, "can't you tell me where she has gone?"

"She rented a room from me," said the woman pensively, as she bitterly reflected on Margot's ingratitude in hiding from her both the rich friend and her new address, though there had not been much difficulty in sniffing out the latter.

"What can I do?" exclaimed Albinus. "Can't you suggest anything?"

Yes, sadly ungrateful. She had helped her so; now she did not quite know whether by telling she would be doing Margot a service or the reverse (she would have preferred the second), but this big, nervous, blue-eyed gentleman looked so unhappy that with a sigh she told him what he wanted to know.

"They used to be after me, too, in the old days," she muttered, nodding her head, while she let him out, "that they did."

It was half past seven. Lights were being put on, and their soft orange glow looked very lovely in the pale dusk. The sky was still quite blue, with a single salmon-colored cloud in the distance, and all this unsteady balance between light and dusk made Albinus feel giddy.

"In another moment I shall be in paradise," he thought, as he sped in a taxi over the whispering asphalt.

Three tall poplars grew in front of the big brick house where she now lived. A brand-new brass plate with her name was affixed to her door. A huge female with arms like lumps of raw meat went to announce him. "Got a cook already," he thought lovingly. "Walk in," said the cook, coming back. He smoothed down his sparse hair and went in.

Margot was lying in a kimono on a dreadful

chintz-covered sofa, her arms crossed behind her head. On her stomach an open book was poised, cover upward.

"You're quick," she said, languidly extending her hand.

"Why, you don't seem surprised to see me," he murmured softly. "Guess how I found out your address."

"I wrote you my address," she said with a sigh, raising both elbows again.

"It was rather amusing," Albinus continued without heeding her words—just gloating over the sight of the painted lips which in another moment . . . "Rather amusing—especially as you've been pulling my leg with that ready-made aunt of yours."

"Why did you go there?" inquired Margot, suddenly very cross. "I wrote you my address— in the top right-hand corner, quite clearly."

"Top corner? Clearly?" repeated Albinus, puckering up his face perplexedly. "What on earth are you talking about?"

She shut the book with a bang and sat up on the couch.

"Surely you got my letter?"

"What letter?" asked Albinus—and suddenly he put his hand to his mouth and his eyes opened very wide.

"I sent you a letter this morning," she said, settling down again and gazing at him curiously. "I reckoned you'd get it by the evening post and come to see me straightaway."

"You didn't!" cried Albinus.

"Of course, I did. And I can tell you exactly what it was I wrote: 'Darling Albert, the wee nest is ready, and birdie is waiting for you. Only don't hug me too hard, or you'll turn your baby's head more than ever.' That's about all."

"Margot," he whispered hoarsely, "Margot, what have you done? I left home before I could possibly get it. The postman . . . he doesn't come until a quarter to eight. It's now—"

"Well, that's no fault of mine," she said. "Really, you are hard to please. It was such a sweet letter."

She shrugged her shoulders, picked up the book and turned her back to him. On the right-hand page was a photographic study of Greta Garbo.

Albinus found himself thinking: "How strange. A disaster occurs and still a man notices a picture." Twenty minutes to eight. Margot lay there, her body curved and motionless, like a lizard.

"You've shattered . . ." he began at the top of his voice; but he did not end his sentence. He ran out, rushed downstairs, jumped into a cab and while he sat on the very edge of the seat leaning forward (winning a few inches that way), he stared at the back of the driver and that back was hopeless.

He arrived, he jumped out, he paid as men do in films—blindly thrusting out a coin. By the garden-railing he saw the familiar figure of the gaunt, knock-kneed postman talking to the short stout hall-porter.

"Any letters for me?" asked Albinus breathlessly.

"I've just delivered them, sir," answered the postman with a friendly grin.

Albinus looked up. The windows of his flat were brightly lit, all of them—an unusual thing. With a tremendous effort he entered the house and began to go upstairs. He reached the first landing—and the second. "Let me explain . . . A young artist in need . . . Not quite right in head, writes love letters to strangers." . . . Nonsense—the game was up.

Before reaching his door, he suddenly turned round and rushed down again. A cat crossed the garden path and slipped nimbly between the iron bars.

Ten minutes later he was back in the room which he had entered so gaily a short while ago.

Margot was still curved on the couch in the same posture—a torpid lizard. The book was still open at the same page. Albinus sat down at a little distance from her and began to crack his finger joints.

"Don't do that," said Margot without raising her head.

He stopped, but soon began again.

"Well, has the letter come?"

"Oh, Margot," he said, and cleared his throat several times. "Too late, too late," he cried in a new shrill voice.

He rose, walked up and down the room, blew his nose and sat down on the chair again.

"She reads all my letters," he said, gazing through a moist haze at the toe of his shoe and trying to fit it into the trembling pattern of the carpet.

"Well, you ought to have forbidden her to do that."

"Margot, you don't understand . . . It was always like that—a habit, a pleasure. Mislaid them sometimes before I had read them. There were all sorts of amusing letters. How could you do it? I can't imagine what she'll do now. If, by a miracle, just this once . . . perhaps she was busy with something . . . perhaps . . . No!"

"Well, mind you don't show yourself when

she comes along here. I'll see her alone, in the hall."

"Who? When?" he asked, dully remembering the drunken hag he had seen—ages ago.

"When? Any moment, I suppose. She's got my address now, hasn't she?"

Albinus still failed to understand.

"Oh, that's what you mean," he muttered at last. "How silly you are, Margot! Believe me, that, at any rate, is utterly impossible. Anything else . . . but not that."

"So much the better," thought Margot, and suddenly she felt extremely elated. When she had sent off the letter she had anticipated a far more trivial consequence: he refuses to show it, wife gets wild, stamps, has a fit. So the first suspicions are roused and that eases the way. But now chance had helped her and the way was made clear at one stroke. She let the book slip to the floor and smiled as she looked at his downcast twitching face. It was time to act, she supposed.

Margot stretched herself out, was aware of a pleasant tingling in her slim body and said, gazing up at the ceiling, "Come here."

He came, sat down on the edge of the couch and shook his head despondently.

"Kiss me," she said, closing her eyes. "I'll comfort you."

82

∞§ 9 §∞

BERLIN-WEST, a morning in May. Men in white caps cleaning the street. Who are they who leave old patent leather boots in the gutter? Sparrows bustling about in the ivy. An electric milk van on fat tires rolling creamily. The sun dazzling in an attic window on the slope of a green-tiled roof. The young fresh air itself was not yet used to the hooting of the distant traffic; it gently took up the sounds and bore them along like something fragile and precious. In the front gardens the Persian lilac was in bloom. Despite the early coolness white butterflies were already fluttering about as though in a rustic garden. All these things surrounded Albinus as he walked out of the house in which he had spent the night.

He was conscious of a dull discomfort. He was hungry; he had neither shaved nor bathed; the touch of yesterday's shirt against his skin was exasperating. He felt utterly spent—and no won-

83

der. This had been the night of which he had dreamed for years. The very way in which she had drawn her shoulder blades together and purred when he first kissed her downy back had told him that he would get exactly what he wanted, and what he wanted was not the chill of innocence. As in his most reckless visions, everything was permissible; a puritan's love, priggish reserve, was less known in this new free world than white bears in Honolulu.

Her nudity was as natural as though she had long been wont to run along the shore of his dreams. There was something delightfully acrobatic about her bed manners. And afterward she would skip out and prance up and down the room, swinging her girlish hips and gnawing at a dry roll left over from supper.

She fell asleep quite suddenly, as though she had stopped speaking in the middle of a sentence, when the electric light was already turning a death-cell yellow and the window a ghostly blue. He made his way into the bathroom, but only a few drops of rust-colored water could be coaxed from the tap. He sighed, picked a dejected loofah out of the bath with two fingers, dropped it gingerly, examined the slippery pink soap and reflected that he must instruct Margot in the rules of cleanliness. His teeth chattering, he dressed;

spread the eiderdown over Margot, who was sweetly sleeping, kissed her warm, tousled dark hair, left a penciled note on the table and stepped softly out.

Now, as he strolled along in the mild sunshine, he realized that the reckoning was about to begin. When he saw again the house in which he had lived for so long with Elisabeth; when he went up in the lift in which the nurse with his baby in her arms, and his wife, looking very pale and happy, had gone up eight years before; when he stood before the door upon which his scholarly name gleamed sedately, Albinus was almost prepared to renounce any repetition of the previous night, if only a miracle had happened. He was sure that if Elisabeth had not read the letter, he would be able to explain his absence somehow— he might say he had tried, in jest, smoking opium at the rooms of that Japanese artist who had once come to dinner—that would be quite plausible.

But now he had to open this door, walk in and see . . . What would he see? . . . Would it not be best perhaps, not to enter at all—just to leave everything as it was, to desert, to vanish?

Suddenly he remembered how, during the War, he had forced himself not to stoop too much when leaving cover.

In the hall he stood motionless, listening. Not

a sound. Usually at this hour of the morning the flat was full of noises: somewhere water would be running, the nurse would be talking loudly to Irma, the maid rattling crockery in the dining room. . . . Not a sound! In the corner stood Elisabeth's umbrella. He tried to find some comfort in that. All at once, as he stood there, Frieda, apronless, appeared from the passage, stared at him, and then said wretchedly:

"Oh, sir, they all went away last night."

"Where?" asked Albinus, not looking at her.

She told him everything. She spoke fast and unusually loudly. Then she burst into tears as she took his hat and stick.

"Will you have some coffee?" she wailed.

The disorder in the bedroom told its tale. His wife's evening gowns lay on the bed. One drawer of the chest was pulled out. The little portrait of his late father-in-law had vanished from the table. The corner of the rug was turned up.

Albinus turned it back and walked quietly to the study. Some opened letters lay on the desk. Ah, there it was—what childish handwriting! Bad spelling, bad spelling. An invitation for lunch from the Dreyers. How nice. A short letter from Rex. The dentist's bill. Splendid.

Two hours later Paul appeared. I see he has

shaved himself clumsily. Crisscross on his plump cheek was some black sticking plaster.

"I've come for the things," he said as he went by.

Albinus followed him, jingling coins in his trousers pocket and looked on in silence while he and Frieda hastily packed the trunk as though they were in a hurry to catch a train.

"Don't forget the umbrella," said Albinus vaguely.

Then he followed them again and the packing was repeated in the nursery. In the Fräulein's room a portmanteau stood ready. They took that too.

"Paul, just a word," murmured Albinus and he cleared his throat and went into the study. Paul came in and stood by the window.

"This is a tragedy," said Albinus.

"Let me tell you one thing," exclaimed Paul at length, staring out of the window. "It will be exceedingly lucky if Elisabeth survives the shock. She—"

He broke off. The black cross on his cheek went up and down.

"She's like a dead woman, as it is. You have . . . You are . . . In fact, you're a scoundrel, sir, an absolute scoundrel."

"Aren't you being rather rude?" said Albinus, trying to smile.

"It's monstrous!" shouted Paul, looking at his brother-in-law for the first time. "Where did you pick her up? How did this prostitute dare to write to you?"

"Gently, gently," said Albinus, and licked his lips.

"I'll thrash you, I'm hanged if I don't!" shouted Paul still louder.

"Remember Frieda," muttered Albinus. "She can hear every word."

"Will you give me an answer?"—and Paul tried to catch hold of the lapel of his coat, but Albinus with a sickly grin slapped him on the hand.

"I refuse to be cross-examined," he whispered. "All this is extremely painful. Can't you think it's some dreadful misunderstanding? Suppose—"

"You're lying!" roared Paul, thumping the floor with a chair, "you cad! I've just been to see her. A little harlot, who ought to be in a reformatory. I knew you'd lie, you cad. How could you do such a thing? This is not mere vice, it's . . ."

"That's enough," Albinus interrupted almost inaudibly.

A motor lorry drove past; the window panes rattled slightly.

"Oh, Albert," said Paul, in an unexpectedly calm and melancholy tone, "who would have thought it . . ."

He went out. Frieda was sobbing in the wings. Someone carried out the luggage. Then all was silent.

৺§ 10 ৡ৹

THAT afternoon Albinus packed his suitcase and drove to Margot's rooms. It had not been easy to persuade Frieda to remain in the empty flat, Finally she agreed when he proposed that her young man, a worthy police-sergeant, should occupy what had been the nurse's bedroom. And if anyone rang up she was to say that Albinus had unexpectedly left for Italy with his family.

Margot received him coldly. That morning she had been roused by a fat irate gentleman who was looking for his brother-in-law; he had called her names. The cook, a particularly hefty woman, had pushed him out, thank goodness!

"This flat is really only meant for one person," she said, glancing at Albinus' suitcase.

"Oh, please," he murmured miserably.

"Anyway there's a lot of things we must talk about. I've no intention of listening to the insults of your idiotic relations"—and she walked up and down the room in her red silk wrapper, her right hand at her left armpit, and puffed hard at a cigarette. With her dark hair falling over her brow she looked like a gypsy.

After tea she drove off to buy a gramophone. Why a gramophone? On this of all days . . . Utterly exhausted and with a splitting headache, Albinus lay on the sofa in the hideous drawing room and thought: "Something unspeakably awful has happened, but I'm really quite calm. Elisabeth's swoon lasted twenty minutes, and then she screamed; probably it was terrible to hear her; and I'm quite calm. She is still my wife and I love her, and I shall, of course, shoot myself if she dies by my fault. I wonder how they explained to Irma the move to Paul's flat and all the hurry and upset? It was disgusting the way Frieda described it: 'and madam screamed, and madam screamed.' . . . Odd, because Elisabeth had never raised her voice before in her life."

The next day, while Margot was out buying records, he wrote a long letter. In this he assured his wife quite sincerely, although maybe in too florid a style, that he treasured her as before, despite his little escapade "which has bruised our family happiness as the knife of a madman slashes a picture." He wept, listened to make sure that Margot was not coming back and wrote on, sobbing and muttering to himself. He begged his wife's forgiveness, but his letter gave no indication as to whether he was prepared to give up his mistress.

He received no answer.

Then he realized that, if he was not to go on tormenting himself, he must erase the image of his family from his memory and abandon himself utterly to the fierce, almost morbid passion which Margot's gay loveliness excited in him. She on her part was always ready to respond to his love-making; it only refreshed her; she was playful and without a care; the doctor had told her two years before that she could never have a child, and she regarded this as a boon and a blessing.

Albinus taught her to bathe daily instead of only washing her hands and neck as she had done hitherto. Her nails were always clean now, and polished a brilliant red, on both fingers and toes.

He kept discovering new charms in her—touching little things which in any other girl would have seemed to him coarse and vulgar. The childish lines of her body, her shamelessness and the gradual dimming of her eyes (as if they were being slowly extinguished like the lights in a theater) roused him to such frenzy that he lost the last vestige of that diffidence which his prim and delicate wife had demanded of his embraces.

92

He hardly ever left the house for fear of meeting acquaintances. It was with reluctance, and only in the mornings, that he let Margot go out— on her adventurous hunts after stockings and silk underwear. He was amazed at her lack of curiosity: she never questioned him about his former life. Sometimes he tried to interest her in his past, telling her of his childhood, his mother whom he remembered but vaguely, and his father, a full-blooded country squire, who had loved well his dogs and horses, his oaks and his corn, and who had died quite suddenly—of a fit of virile laughter in the billiard room where a guest was telling a bawdy story.

"What was the story? Tell it to me," Margot asked—but he had forgotten it.

He told her about his early passion for painting, his works, his discoveries; he told her how a picture could be restored with the aid of garlic and crushed resin which converted the old varnish into dust and how, under a flannel rag moistened with turpentine, the smokiness or the coarse picture painted over would vanish and the original beauty blossom out.

Margot was chiefly interested in the market value of such a picture.

He told her about the War, and the cold mud of the trenches, and she asked him why, being

93

rich, he had not wangled himself into a post behind the lines.

"What a funny darling you are!" he would cry, fondling her.

She began to get bored in the evenings; she longed for the cinema, smart restaurants and negroid music.

"You shall have everything, everything," he said, "only let me recover first. I have all sorts of plans. . . . We'll go to the seaside soon."

He looked round her drawing room and marveled how he, who prided himself on not being able to endure anything in bad taste, could tolerate this chamber of horrors. Everything, he mused, was beautified by his passion.

"We've really fixed ourselves up very nicely—haven't we, darling?"

She agreed condescendingly. She knew that all this was only temporary: the memory of his luxurious flat lingered in her mind; but of course there was no need for haste.

One day, in July, as Margot was returning from her dressmaker's on foot, and was already nearing home, someone clutched her from behind above the elbow. She wheeled round. It was her brother Otto. He grinned unpleasantly. At a little distance two of his friends were standing and they grinned too.

94

"Glad to meet you, Sis," he said. "Not very nice of you to forget your folks."

"Let go," said Margot quietly, drooping her eyelashes.

Otto stuck his arms akimbo: "How fine you look," he said, examining her from head to foot. "Really, quite the young lady!"

Margot turned round and walked away. But he gripped her arm again, hurting her, and she uttered a soft "Ow-wow!" as she had done when she was a child.

"Look here," said Otto, "this is the third day I've been watching you. I know where you live. But we'd better move on a little farther."

"Let me go," whispered Margot, trying to loosen his fingers. A passer-by stopped, anticipating a row. Her house was quite near. Albinus might happen to look out of the window. That would be a nuisance.

She yielded to his pressure. He led her round the corner; leering and swinging their arms, the other two, Kaspar and Kurt, followed.

"What is it you want?" she asked, gazing with disgust at her brother's greasy cap and at the cigarette behind his ear.

He motioned with his head to one side: "Let's go into the bar there."

"No," she cried, but the other two came close

95

up to her and snarled as they shoved her toward the door. She began to feel frightened.

At the bar a few men were discussing the coming elections in loud barking tones.

"Let's sit here, in this corner," said Otto.

They sat down. Margot remembered vividly and with a kind of wonder how they all used to go out on suburban sprees—she, Otto, and these two sun-tanned youths. They taught her to swim and grabbed at her bared thighs under the water. Kurt had an anchor tattooed on his forearm and a dragon on his chest. They sprawled on the bank and pelted one another with clammy velvety sand. They slapped her on her wet bathing pants as soon as she lay down flat. How jolly it all was, the merry crowd, litter of paper everywhere, and muscular, fair-haired Kaspar on the edge of the lake shaking his arms as though he were quaking, and roaring: "The water is wet, wet!" When swimming, he held his mouth under water and trumpeted like a seal. And when he came out, the first thing he did was to comb back his hair and carefully put on his cap. She remembered how they played ball; and then she lay down and they covered her with sand leaving only her face bare, and made a cross of pebbles on top.

"See here," said Otto, when four gold-rimmed

glasses of light beer appeared on the table. "You've no need to be ashamed of your people because you've got a rich friend. On the contrary, you must think about us." He took a sip, and his friends did the same. They both watched Margot with contemptuous hostility.

"You don't know what you're talking about," she said disdainfully. "It's quite different from what you think. As a matter of fact we're engaged."

All three burst out laughing. Margot was filled with such loathing that she looked away and fidgeted with the fastening of her handbag. Otto took it out of her hand, opened it and found there a powder-box, keys, a tiny handkerchief and three and a half marks, which he took.

"That'll be enough for the beer," he remarked, then he made a little bow and laid the bag in front of her.

They ordered more. Margot, too, swallowed some with an effort: she hated beer, but she did not want them to have hers.

"Can I go now?" she asked, patting the twin locks on her temples.

"What? Don't you like sitting with your brother and his friends?" asked Otto in mock astonishment. "My dear, you've changed a lot. But—we've not yet come to business . . ."

"You've stolen my money, and now I'm going."

Again they all snarled and again she felt frightened.

"No question of stealing," said Otto nastily. "This isn't your money, but money which you got hold of from someone who sweated it out of the working classes. So you'd better not talk about stealing. You—"

He checked himself and continued more calmly:

"Listen here, you. Get some cash from your friend for us, for the family. Fifty will do. See?"

"And suppose I don't?"

"Then we'll have our sweet revenge," answered Otto quietly. "Oh, we know all about you. Engaged! That's a good one."

Margot beamed suddenly and whispered with lowered eyelashes:

"All right, I'll get it. Is that all? Can I go now?"

"Good girl. But what's the hurry? Besides, we ought to see a little more of one another. How about taking a trip to the lake one day, eh?" He turned to his friends. "What larks we used to have! She ought not to give herself such airs, ought she?"

But Margot had already risen to her feet and was emptying her glass, standing.

"Noon tomorrow, at the same corner," said Otto, "and then we'll drive out for the whole day. Agreed?"

"Agreed," said Margot brightly. She shook hands all round and went out.

She returned home and when Albinus put down his paper and rose to meet her, she tottered and pretended to faint. It was an indifferent performance, but it worked. He was thoroughly frightened, made her comfortable on the couch, brought her some water.

"What's the matter? Do tell me," he kept repeating, as he stroked her hair.

"Now you'll leave me," groaned Margot.

He gulped and immediately leaped to the worst conclusion: she had been unfaithful to him.

"Good. Then I'll kill her," he thought swiftly. But aloud he repeated quite calmly: "What's the matter, Margot?"

"I have deceived you," she whimpered.

"She must die," thought Albinus.

"I've deceived you terribly, Albert. First of all, my father is not an artist; he used to be a locksmith, and now he's a porter; my mother polishes the banisters, and my brother's a common workman. I had a hard, hard childhood. I was flogged, tortured."

Albinus felt exquisite relief, and then a flood of pity.

"No, don't kiss me. You must know all. I escaped from home. I earned money as a model. A terrible old woman exploited me. Then I had a love affair. He was married like you, and his wife wouldn't divorce him, so I left him, as I could not bear to be only his mistress—although I loved him madly. Then I was pestered by an old banker. He offered his whole fortune to me, but of course I refused him. He died of a broken heart. Then I took that job at the 'Argus.' "

"Oh, my poor, poor, hunted little bunny," murmured Albinus (who, incidentally, had long ceased to believe that he was her first lover).

"And you really don't despise me?" she asked, smiling through her tears, which was difficult, seeing there were no tears to smile through. "I'm so glad you don't despise me. But now let me tell you the most terrible part: my brother has found out where I live, I met him today and he demands money—trying to blackmail me, because he thinks you know nothing—about my past, I mean. You see, when I saw him and thought what a disgrace it was to have such a brother and then when I thought that my sweet trusting woggy had no idea what my family was like—

you know I was so ashamed of them, and because I had not told you the truth, too . . ."

He took her up in his arms and rocked her to and fro; he would have crooned a lullaby had he known one. She began to laugh softly.

"What's to be done about it?" he asked. "I'll be afraid to let you go out alone now. Shall we tell the police?"

"No, not that," exclaimed Margot with extraordinary emphasis.

⋅§ 11 §⋅

NEXT day for the first time Albinus accompanied her when she went out. She wanted many
light frocks and bathing things and pounds of
cream that would help the sun to bronze her.
Solfi, the Adriatic resort which Albinus had selected for their first trip together, was a hot and
dazzling place. As they were getting into a cab,
she noticed her brother standing on the other
side of the street, but she did not point him out
to Albinus.

Showing himself with Margot made him
acutely uncomfortable; he could not get used
to his new position. When they returned, Otto
had vanished. Margot rightly supposed that he
was very hurt and would now act injudiciously.

Two days before their departure Albinus was
seated at a peculiarly uncomfortable desk writing
a business letter while she was packing things
into the new shiny black trunk in the adjoining

room. He heard the rustling of tissue paper and a little song which she was softly humming to herself, her mouth shut.

"How strange it all is," thought he. "Had I been told on New Year's Eve that my life would change so completely in a few months . . ."

Margot dropped something in the next room. The humming stopped for a moment, and was then softly resumed.

"Six months ago I was a model husband in a Margot-less world. Quick work fate made of it! Other men can combine a happy family life with little infidelities, but in my case everything went crash immediately. Why? And here I sit and seem to be thinking clearly and sensibly. Yet in reality the earthquake is in full swing and God knows how things will settle themselves . . ."

Suddenly the bell rang. From three different doors Albinus, Margot and the cook all ran out into the hall simultaneously.

"Albert," whispered Margot, "be very careful. I'm sure it's him."

"Go to your room," he whispered back. "I'll handle him nicely."

He opened the door. It was the girl from the milliner's. Hardly had she gone, than there was another ring. He opened again. Before him stood a youth with a coarse oafish countenance, yet resembling Margot strikingly—those dark eyes, that sleek hair, that straight nose slightly wedged at the tip. He wore his Sunday suit and the end of his tie was tucked into his shirt between the buttons.

"What do you want?" asked Albinus.

Otto coughed and said with a confidential huskiness in his voice:

"I must talk to you about my sister. I'm Margot's brother."

"And why to me particularly, may I ask?"

"You are Herr . . .?" began Otto in a questioning tone. "Herr . . .?"

"Schiffermiller," said Albinus, rather relieved to learn that the boy did not know his identity.

"Well, Herr Schiffermiller, I happened to see you with my sister. So I thought it would perhaps interest you if I . . . if we . . ."

"Certainly—but why stand in the doorway? Please come inside."

He came and coughed again.

"What I want to say is this, Herr Schiffermiller. My sister is young and inexperienced. Mother hasn't slept a single night since our little Margot left home. She's only sixteen, you know—don't believe her if she says she's older. Let me tell you, we're decent people—my father's an old soldier. It's a very, very unpleasant situation. I don't know what amends can be made . . ."

Otto, gaining confidence, was beginning almost to believe what he said.

"I really don't know," he continued with rising excitement. "Just imagine, Herr Schiffermiller, if you had a loved and innocent sister whom someone had bought . . ."

"Now listen, my good fellow," Albinus interrupted him. "There seems to be some mistake. My fiancée told me that her family was only too thankful to be rid of her."

"Oh, no," said Otto winking. "You're not going to make me believe you'll marry her. When a man wants to marry a respectable girl, he talks to her family about it. A little more care and a little less pride, Herr Schiffermiller!"

Albinus gazed at Otto with curiosity, as he reflected that the young brute was talking sense in a way, for he had as much right to concern himself over Margot's welfare as Paul had to worry on behalf of *his* sister. Indeed, there was a fine flavor of parody about this talk, in comparison with that other dreadful conversation two months ago. And it was pleasant to think that now at least he could stand his own ground, brother or no brother—take advantage, as it were, of the fact that Otto was simply a bluffer and a bully.

"You'd better stop," he said, very resolutely, very coolly—quite the patrician, in fact. "I know exactly how things stand. It is no concern of yours. Now please go."

"Oh, really," said Otto frowning. "Very well."

He was silent, twisted his cap in his hand and looked at the floor. Then he tried a different key.

"You may have to pay dearly for it before you've done, Herr Schiffermiller. My little sister is not exactly what you think her to be. I called her innocent, but that was brotherly compassion. You're too easily led by the nose, Herr Schiffermiller. It's mighty funny to hear you call her your fiancée. It makes me laugh. Now, I could tell you a thing or two . . ."

"Quite superfluous," replied Albinus flushing. "She has told me everything herself. An unfortunate child whom her family could not protect. Please, go at once"—and Albinus opened the door.

"You'll regret it," said Otto awkwardly.

"Go or I'll kick you out," said Albinus (putting the last sweet touch to victory, so to speak).

Otto retired very slowly.

Being endowed with that kind of shallow sentimentality peculiar to his bourgeois set, Albinus (with the plum in his mouth) suddenly pictured to himself how poor and ugly the life of this boy must be. Also—he *did* look like Margot, when Margot sulked. Before shutting the door he swiftly produced a ten-mark note and pressed it into Otto's hand.

The door closed. Otto alone on the landing examined the note, stood there a moment lost in thought, then rang the bell.

"What, back again?" exclaimed Albinus.

Otto stretched out his hand with the money.

"I don't want your tips," he muttered angrily. "Better give it to the unemployed—there are plenty of them about."

"But, please take it," said Albinus feeling terribly embarrassed.

Otto shrugged his shoulders.

"I don't accept crumbs from the bloody rich. A poor man has his pride. I . . ."

"Well, it was only meant . . ." began Albinus.

Otto shuffled his feet, thrust the note sullenly into his pocket and, muttering, walked on downstairs. Social honor was satisfied, now he could afford to satisfy more human needs.

"Not much," he reflected, "but better than nothing, anyway—and he's afraid of me, the pop-eyed, stammering fool."

◆§ 12 ◆

FROM the moment when Elisabeth had read Margot's short letter, her life had turned into one of those long grotesque riddles that one is set to work out in the dream classroom of dull delirium. And, at first, she felt as if her husband were dead and people were trying to deceive her into thinking that he had only deserted her.

She remembered how—on that evening which now seemed so remote—she had kissed him on the forehead before he went, and he had said as he stooped: "Anyhow, you had better see Lampert. She can't go on scratching herself like that."

These had been his last words in this life, simple homely words referring to a slight rash which had broken out on Irma's neck—and then he had gone forever.

The zinc ointment had cured the rash in a few days—but there was no ointment in the world which could mollify and erase the memory of his big white forehead and the way he had patted his pockets as he left the room.

During the first days she wept so much that she herself was surprised at the capacity of her lachrymal glands. Do scientists know how much salted water can flow from a person's eyes? And that reminded her of how, one summer on the Italian coast, they had used to bathe the baby in a tub of sea water—oh, one might fill a far bigger tub with her tears, and wash a struggling giant.

Somehow his abandonment of Irma seemed to her far more monstrous than his desertion of her. Or would he be trying to steal his daughter? Was it prudent to have sent her to the country alone with the nurse? It was, said Paul, and he urged her to go there too. But she would not hear of it. Although she felt she could never forgive (not that he had humiliated *her*—she was much too proud to feel wronged that way—but because he had abased himself), still Elisabeth waited on, hoping from day to day that the door would open like the night in a thunderclap and that her husband would come in, pale as Lazarus, his blue eyes swollen and wet, his clothes worn to shreds, his arms wide open.

The greater part of the day she sat in one of the rooms or sometimes even in the hall—in any place where the heavy mists of her thoughts happened to overtake her—and pondered over this or that detail of her married life. It seemed to her he had always been unfaithful. And now she remembered and understood (as one learning a new language might remember once seeing a book in that tongue when one did not yet know it) the red stains—sticky red kisses—which she had noticed once on her husband's pocket handkerchief.

Paul did all he could to distract her thoughts. He never referred to Albinus. He changed some of his pet habits—that of spending Sunday morning at the turkish baths for instance. He brought her magazines and novels; and they talked about their childhood, their parents long dead and that fair-haired brother of theirs who had been killed on the Somme: a musician, a dreamer.

One hot summer day when they had gone to the Park they watched a small monkey which had escaped from its owner and was up in a tall elm tree. Its little black face in a crown of gray fluff peered out of the green leaves, then was gone and a branch rustled and shook several feet higher. In vain did its master try to tempt it down by means of a soft whistle, a large yellow banana, a pocket mirror which he flashed and flashed.

"It won't come back, it's hopeless; it will never come back," she murmured, and burst into tears.

⇜ 13 ⇝

WITH nothing but deep blue above, Margot lay spread-eagled on the platinum sand, her limbs a rich honey-brown, and a thin white rubber belt relieving the black of her bathing-suit: the perfect seaside poster. Lying alongside of her, Albinus propped up his cheek and looked with endless delight at the oily gloss of her closed eyelids and at her freshly made-up mouth. Her wet dark hair was thrown back from her round forehead and grains of sand glittered in her little ears. If you looked very close, there was an iridescent sheen in the pits of her brown polished shoulders. The close-fitting seal-like black thing she had on was much too short to be true.

Albinus let a handful of sand trickle, as from an hour-glass, onto her indrawn stomach. She opened her eyes, blinked in the silver-blue blaze, smiled and shut her eyes again.

After a while she drew herself up, clasped her

arms round her knees and remained sitting motionless. Now he could see her back bared to the waist with the glitter of sand grains along the curve of her spine. He brushed them away gently. Her skin was silky and hot.

"Heavens," said Margot, "how blue the sea is today."

It really was blue: purple-blue in the distance peacock-blue coming nearer, diamond-blue where the wave caught the light. The foam toppled over, ran, slowed down, then receded, leaving a smooth mirror on the wet sand, which the next wave flooded again. A hairy man in orange-red pants stood at the edge of the water wiping his glasses. A small boy shrieked with glee as the foam gushed into the walled city he had built. Gay parasols and striped tents seemed to repeat in terms of color what the shouts of the bathers were to the ear. A large bright ball was flung from somewhere and bounced on the sand with a ringing thud. Margot grabbed it, jumped up and swung it back.

Now Albinus saw her figure framed in the gay pattern of the beach; a pattern he hardly saw, so entirely was his gaze concentrated on Margot. Slim, sunburned, with her dark head of hair and one arm with the gleam of a bracelet still outstretched after her throw, she seemed to him an exquisitely colored vignette heading the first chapter of his new life.

She went up to him as he lay full-length (a towel over his pink blistered shoulders), watching the movements of her little feet. She bent over him and, with a Berlinese chuckle, gave him a nice hard slap on his well-filled bathing pants.

"The water is wet!" she cried, and ran into the surf. There she advanced swinging her hips and her outspread arms, pushing forward in knee-deep water, then fell on all fours, tried to swim, gurgled, scrambled up and went on, up to the waist in foam. He splashed in after her. She turned toward him, laughing, spitting, wiping the wet hair from her eyes. He attempted to duck her, then caught her by the ankle and she kicked and screamed.

An Englishwoman who was lolling in a deck-chair beneath a mauve sunshade reading *Punch* turned to her husband, a red-faced, white-hatted man squatting on the sand, and said:

"Look at that German romping about with his daughter. Now, don't be so lazy, William. Take the children out for a good swim."

114

◂§ 14 §▸

AFTERWARD, in their gaudy bathgowns, they walked up and up a flinty path, half-smothered in broom and ulex. Yonder a small villa, whose rent was enormous, gleamed white as sugar between the black cypresses. Great, beautiful crickets skidded across the gravel. Margot tried to catch them. She crouched down and cautiously stretched out finger and thumb, but the cricket's sharp-elbowed limbs jerked suddenly, the fan-shaped blue wings shot out and it flew three yards on to vanish as soon as it fell.

In the cool room with the red-tiled floor, where the light through the slits of the shutters danced in one's eyes and lay in bright lines at one's feet, Margot, snake-like, shuffled off her black skin, and, with nothing on but high-heeled slippers, clicked up and down the room, eating a sibilant peach; and stripes of sunshine crossed and re-crossed her body.

In the evenings, there was dancing at the casino. The sea looked paler than the flushed sky, and the lights of a passing steamer glowed festively. A clumsy moth flapped round a rose-shaded lamp; and Albinus danced with Margot. Her smoothly brushed head barely reached his shoulder.

Very soon after their arrival they made several acquaintances. He was conscious of a gnawing degrading jealousy when he saw how closely Margot pressed to her partner as she danced, especially as he knew that she had nothing on beneath her flimsy frock: her legs had browned so prettily that she wore no stockings. Sometimes Albinus lost sight of her. Then he got up and walked about restlessly, tapping a cigarette against his case. He would wander into a room where people were playing cards, and onto a terrace, and then back again with the sickening conviction that she was deceiving him. Suddenly she would appear from nowhere and sit down by his side in her beautiful, shimmering dress and take a long draught of wine. He did not betray his fears, but nervously stroked beneath the table her bare knees which knocked against one another as she leaned back in her chair and laughed—a little hysterically, he thought—at something—not overfunny—that her latest partner was saying.

To Margot's credit it must be admitted that
she did try her utmost to remain quite faithful
to him. But no matter how tender and thought-
ful he was in his love-making, she knew, all along,
that for her it would always be love minus something, whereas the least touch of her first lover
had always been a sample of everything. Unfortunately a young Austrian who was the best dancer
in Solfi, and a crack ping-pong player to boot,
somehow resembled the man Miller; there was
something about his strong knuckles, his keen
sardonic eyes, which kept reminding her of
things she would have preferred to forget.

One hot night between two dances she happened to stray with him into a dark corner of the
casino garden. The dull sweetish smell of a fig
tree weighted the air and there was that banal
blend of moonlight and distant music which is
apt to affect simple souls.

"No, no," muttered Margot when she felt his
lips on her neck and cheek, while his clever hands
groped their way up her legs.

"You shouldn't," she whispered, and threw
back her head and greedily returned his kiss. He
caressed her so thoroughly that she felt the little
strength she still had ebbing away; but in time
she slipped free and ran to the brightly lit terrace.

This scene was never repeated. Margot had

so fallen in love with the life that Albinus could offer her—a life full of the glamour of a first-class film with rocking palm trees and shuddering roses (for it is always windy in filmland) —and she was so afraid of seeing it all snap that she dared not take any risks; indeed, she even lost for a time her ruling characteristic—self-confidence. She recovered it, however, as soon as they returned to Berlin in the autumn.

"Very nice, to be sure," she said drily as she surveyed the good hotel room where they had put up, "but I hope you understand, Albert, that we can't go on like this forever."

Albinus, who was dressing for dinner, hastened to assure her that he was already taking steps to rent a new flat.

"Does he really think me a fool?" she wondered with fierce resentment.

"Albert," she said aloud, "I see you don't understand." She sighed deeply and covered her face with her hands. "You're ashamed of me," she said, watching him through her fingers.

Gaily he tried to embrace her.

"Don't touch me," she screamed, giving him a smart shove with her elbow. "I know perfectly well you're afraid to be seen with me in the street. If you're ashamed of me, you can leave me and go back to your Lizzy. You're quite free."

118

"Don't, darling," he pleaded helplessly.

She flung herself on the sofa and managed to burst into sobs.

Albinus pulled up the knees of his trousers, knelt down, and tried carefully to touch her shoulder, which jerked every time his fingers approached it.

"What is it you want?" he asked softly. "What is it you want, Margot?"

"I want to live with you quite openly," she blubbered. "In your own home. And to see people . . ."

"Very well," he said, rising to his feet and brushing his knees.

("And in a year's time you'll marry me," thought Margot as she went on sobbing nicely, "you'll marry me unless by that time I'm already in Hollywood—in which case you may go to the devil.")

"If you don't stop crying," said Albinus, "I shall begin to cry myself."

Margot sat up and smiled plaintively. Tears only added to her beauty. Her face was aflame, the iris of her eyes was dazzling, and a large tear trembled on the side of her nose: he had never before seen tears of that size and brilliance.

❧ 15 ❧

JUST as Albinus had accustomed himself never
to speak to Margot of art, of which she knew and
cared nothing, he had now to learn to hide from
her the agonies he suffered during the first days of
their life together in the old flat, where he had
spent ten years with his wife. All around were
objects which reminded him of Elisabeth; her
presents to him and his to her. In Frieda's eyes
he read sullen censure, and, before a week had
passed, she left after listening contemptuously to
Margot's second or third outburst of shrill
scolding.

The bedroom and the nursery seemed to gaze at
Albinus with touching and innocent reproach—
especially the bedroom; for Margot had promptly
cleared everything out of the nursery and turned
it into a ping-pong room. But the bedroom . . .
The first night Albinus fancied he could detect
the faint scent of his wife's eau-de-Cologne, and

this depressed and hampered him, so that Margot giggled over his unexpected reserve.

The first telephone call was torture. An old friend rang up to ask if they had had a good time in Italy, how Elisabeth was feeling and whether she could go with his wife to a concert on Sunday morning.

"As a matter of fact, we are living apart for the present," Albinus said with an effort. ("For the present!" thought Margot mockingly, as she twisted before the mirror to examine her back which had faded from brown to golden.)

The news of the change in his life very soon spread, though he fondly hoped nobody knew that his mistress lived with him; he took the usual precaution, when they began to have parties, which was to have Margot go off with the other guests—and come back ten minutes later.

He felt a dismal interest in noticing the way people gradually stopped inquiring after his wife; how some ceased to visit him; how a few, the staunch borrowers, were surprisingly friendly and hearty; how the Bohemian crowd tried to look as if nothing had happened; finally, there were some—fellow-scholars mostly—who were ready to visit him as before, but never came with their wives, among whom there seemed to have spread a remarkable epidemic of headaches.

121

He grew accustomed to Margot's presence in these rooms, once so full of memories. She had only to change the position of some trifling object, and immediately it lost its soul and the memory was extinguished; it was only a matter of how long she would take to touch everything, and, as she had quick fingers, in a couple of months his past life in these twelve rooms was quite dead. Beautiful as the flat was, it no longer had anything in common with that flat in which he had lived with his wife.

Late one night, as he was soaping Margot's back after a dance and she was amusing herself by standing in the full bath upon her enormous sponge (bubbles coming up as in a glass of champagne), she suddenly asked him whether he did not think she could become a film actress. He laughed and said thoughtlessly, his mind wholly absorbed in other pleasant things: "Of course, why not?"

A few days later she returned to the subject, this time choosing a moment when Albinus' head was clearer. He was delighted at her interest in the cinema and began to unfold a certain favorite theory of his regarding the comparative merits of the silent film and the talkie: "Sound," he said, "will kill the cinema straightaway."

122

"How do they make a film of you?" she interrupted.

He suggested taking her to a studio where he could show her everything and explain the process. After that things moved very rapidly.

"Stop, what am I doing?" Albinus asked himself one morning, as he recalled that the night before he had promised to finance a film which a mediocre producer wanted to make, on condition that Margot was given the second feminine part, that of a forsaken sweetheart.

"Silly of me!" he thought. "The place will be full of slick young actors dripping with sex-appeal —and I shall make myself ridiculous if I accompany her everywhere. On the other hand," he consoled himself, "she needs some sort of occupation to keep her amused, and if she's going to get up early we'll quit spending every blessed night at dances."

The contract was signed and rehearsals began. For the first two days Margot came home extremely cross and resentful. She complained that she was forced to repeat the same movement hundreds of times in succession; that the director shouted at her; that she was blinded by the lamps. She had only one consolation: the (fairly well-known) actress who was the leading lady,

Dorianna Karenina, was charming to her, praised her acting and prophesied that she would do wonders. ("A bad sign!" thought Albinus.)

She insisted that he should not be present during work: it made her self-conscious, she said. Besides, if he had seen it all beforehand, the film would not be a surprise for him—and Margot liked people to have surprises. However, he derived a great deal of pleasure from catching glimpses of her assuming dramatic poses in front of the cheval glass; a creaking board gave him away, she hurled a red cushion at him and he had to swear he had seen nothing.

He used to take her to the studio in a car and then fetch her home. One day, he was told that the rehearsal would last some two hours, so he went for a walk and blundered into the neighborhood where Paul lived. All at once he felt a keen desire to meet his pale, plain little daughter: it was about the time she usually came back from school. As he turned the corner, he half fancied that he saw her in the distance with her nurse, but suddenly he felt frightened and walked quickly away.

On this particular day Margot came out to him flushed and laughing: she had acted beautifully, beautifully—and soon the filming would be over.

"I'll tell you what," said Albinus. "I'll invite

Dorianna to supper. We'll have a big supper and some interesting guests. Yesterday an artist rang me up, a cartoonist, to be correct, a man who makes funny drawings and things, you know. He's just back from New York, and is quite a genius in his way. I'll get him along too."

"Only I want to sit by you," said Margot.

"All right, but remember, my pet, I don't want them all to know that you live with me."

"Oh, they all know that, you fool," said Margot, her face suddenly darkening.

"But that places you, and not me, in a false position," Albinus pointed out. "You must realize that. It doesn't matter to me, of course, but for your sake, please, do as you did last time."

"But it's so stupid. . . . And besides, there's a way we could avoid these unpleasantnesses."

"How—avoid them?"

"If you don't understand," she pouted. ("When will he begin to talk of the divorce?" she thought.)

"Do be reasonable," said Albinus coaxingly. "I do everything you ask. You know quite well, pussy—"

He had gradually got together quite a little menagerie of pet names.

❧ 16 ☙

EVERYTHING was as it should be. On the lacquer tray in the hall cards had been shrewdly prepared with the names of the expected guests coupled, so that people might know at once with whom they would go in to supper: Dr. Lampert and Sonia Hirsch; Axel Rex and Margot Peters; Boris von Ivanoff and Olga Waldheim—and so on. An impressive footman (recently engaged) with the face of an English lord (or, at any rate, so Margot thought, and her eyes used to linger on him not unkindly) showed in the guests with dignity. Every few minutes the bell rang. In the drawing room there were already five besides Margot. In came Ivanoff—von Ivanoff, as he deemed fit to have himself called—lean, ferrety, with bad teeth and an eyeglass. Then—Baum, the author, a stout, red-faced, fussy-individual with strong communistic leanings and a comfortable income, accompanied by his wife, an elderly woman, her figure still glorious, who, in her troubled youth, had swum about in a glass tank among performing seals.

Conversation was already quite lively. Olga Waldheim, a white-armed, full-bosomed singer, with waved hair the color of orange marmalade and with a gem of melody in every inflection of her voice, was telling, as she usually did, cute stories about her six Persian cats. Albinus, as he stood and laughed, gazed across old Lampert's white brush of hair (a fine throat-specialist and an indifferent violinist) at Margot, and thought how well her black tulle gown with the velvet dahlia at her breast suited her, the darling. There was a faintly defensive smile on her bright lips, as if she were not quite sure whether her leg was being pulled, and her eyes had that special fawn-like expression which meant, he knew, that she was listening to things she did not understand, in this case, Lampert's ideas about Hindemith's music.

Suddenly he noticed that she had blushed violently and risen to her feet. "How foolish—why does she get up?" he thought, as several new guests entered—Dorianna Karenina, Axel Rex and two minor poets.

Dorianna embraced and kissed Margot, whose eyes were shining as brilliantly as if she had just been crying. "How foolish," thought Albinus again, "to grovel before that second-rate actress." Dorianna was famous for her exquisite shoulders, her Mona Lisa smile and her husky grenadier voice.

Albinus walked up to Rex, who did not quite know which was his host and was rubbing his hands as though he were soaping them.

"Delighted to see you at last," said Albinus. "Do you know, I had formed quite a different picture of you in my mind—short, fat, with horn-rimmed glasses, though on the other hand your name always reminds me of an axe. Ladies and gentlemen, this is the man who makes two continents laugh. Let us hope he is back in Germany for good."

Rex, his eyes twinkling, made little bows, rubbing his hands all the time. He sported a striking lounge suit in a world of badly cut German dinner jackets.

"Please, be seated," said Albinus.

"Haven't I met your sister once?" queried Dorianna in her lovely bass voice.

"My sister is in Heaven," answered Rex gravely.

"Oh, I'm sorry," said Dorianna.

"Never was born," he added—and sat down on a chair next to Margot.

Laughing pleasantly, Albinus let his eyes stray back to her. She was bending toward her neighbor, Sonia Hirsch, the plain-faced, motherly cubist, in a queer childlike attitude, her shoulders a little hunched and talking unusually fast, with moist eyes and fluttering eyelids. He looked down at her small, flushed ear, the vein on her neck, the delicate shadow between her breasts. Hurriedly, feverishly, she was pouring out a stream of complete nonsense, with her hand pressed to her flaming cheek.

"Menservants steal far less," she jabbered, "though, of course, no one would lift a really big picture, and at one time I adored big ones with men on horseback, but when one sees such a lot of pictures—"

"Fräulein Peters," said Albinus in a soothing tone, "this is the man who makes two continents—"

Margot started and swerved round.

"Oh, really, how do you do?"

Rex bowed and, turning to Albinus, remarked quietly:

"I happened to read on the boat your excellent biography of Sebastiano del Piombo. Pity, though, you didn't quote his sonnets."

"Oh, but they are very poor," answered Albinus.

"Exactly," said Rex. "That's what is so charming."

Margot jumped up and with swift, almost bounding steps dashed toward the last guest—a long-limbed, withered female, who looked like a plucked eagle. Margot had taken elocution lessons with her.

Sonia Hirsch shifted to Margot's place and turned to Rex:

"What d'you think of Cumming's work?" she asked. "I mean, his last series—the Gallows and Factories, you know?"

"Rotten," said Rex.

The door of the dining room opened. The gentlemen looked round for their ladies. Rex stood aloof. His host, who already had Dorianna on his arm, gazed about in search of Margot. He saw her right in front squeezing among the couples who were streaming into the dining room.

"She is not at her best tonight," he thought anxiously, and handed over his lady to Rex.

By the time the lobsters were being tackled, the talk at the head of the table where (the following string of names would be best arranged in a curve) Dorianna, Rex, Margot, Albinus, Sonia Hirsch and Baum were seated was in full swing although rather incoherent. Margot had emptied her third wineglass at one gulp and was now sitting very erect with bright eyes, staring straight in front of her. Rex paid no attention either to her or to Dorianna, whose name annoyed him, but was arguing across the table with Baum, the author, concerning the means of artistic expression.

"A writer for instance," he remarked, "talks about India which I have never seen, and gushes about dancing girls, tiger hunts, fakirs, betel nuts, serpents: the Glamour of the mysterious East. But what does it amount to? Nothing. Instead of visualizing India I merely get a bad toothache from all these Eastern delights. Now, there's the other way as, for instance, the fellow who writes: 'Before turning in I put out my wet boots to dry and in the morning I found that a thick blue forest had grown on them' ("Fungi, Madam," he explained to Dorianna who had raised one eyebrow) and at once India becomes alive for me. The rest is shop."

"Those yogis do marvelous things," said Dorianna. "Apparently they can breathe in such a way that—"

"But excuse me, my good sir," cried Baum excitedly—for he had just written a five-hundred-page novel, the scene of which was laid in Ceylon, where he had spent a sun-helmeted fortnight.

"You must illuminate the picture thoroughly, so that every reader can understand. What matters is not the book one writes, but the problem it sets —and solves. If I describe the tropics I'm bound to approach my subject from its most important side, and that is—the exploitation, the cruelty of the white colonist. When you think of the millions and millions—"

"I don't," said Rex.

Margot, who was staring in front of her, giggled suddenly—and this, somehow, had nothing to do with the conversation. Albinus, in the middle of discussing the latest art exhibition with the motherly cubist, glanced sideways at his young mistress. Yes, she was drinking too much. Even as he looked, she took a sip out of his own glass. "What a child!" he thought, touching her knee under the table. Margot giggled again and flung a carnation across the table at old Lampert.

"I don't know, gentlemen, what you think of Udo Conrad," said Albinus, joining in the fray. "It would seem to me that he is that type of author with exquisite vision and a divine style which might please you, Herr Rex, and that if he isn't a great writer it is because—and here, Herr Baum, I am with you—he has a contempt for social problems which, in this age of social upheavals, is disgraceful and, let me add, sinful. I knew him well in my student days, as we were together at Heidelberg, and afterward we used to meet now and then. I consider his best book to be *The Vanishing Trick*, the first chapter of which, as a matter of fact, he read here, at this table—I mean—well—at a similar table, and . . ."

After supper they lolled and smoked and drank liqueurs. Margot flitted from place to place and one of the minor poets followed her like a shaggy dog. She suggested burning a hole in his palm with her cigarette and started doing so and, though perspiring freely, he kept smiling like the little hero he was. Rex, who had at length been impossibly offensive to Baum in a corner of the library, now joined Albinus and began to describe to him certain aspects of Berlin as if it were a distant picturesque city; he did it so well that Albinus promised to look up, in his company, that lane, that bridge, that queer-colored wall . . .

"I'm dreadfully sorry," he said, "that we can't get to work together on my film idea. I'm sure you'd have achieved wonders, but to be quite frank I cannot afford it—not just now, at any rate."

At length the guests were caught in that wave which, beginning as a low murmur, swells until, in a whirl of foamy farewells, it has swept them out of the house.

Albinus was left alone. The air was blue and heavy with cigar smoke. Somebody had spilled something on the Turkish table—it was all sticky. The solemn, though slightly unsteady, footman ("If he gets drunk again, I'll dismiss him") opened the window, and the black clear frosty night streamed in.

"Not a very successful party, somehow," thought Albinus as he yawned himself out of his dinner jacket.

✑ 17 ੩

"A CERTAIN man," said Rex, as he turned round the corner with Margot, "once lost a diamond cuff-link in the wide blue sea, and twenty years later, on the exact day, a Friday apparently, he was eating a large fish—but there was no diamond inside. That's what I like about coincidence."

Margot trotted along by his side with her sealskin coat wrapped tightly around her. Rex seized her by the elbow and forced her to come to a halt.

"I never expected to run across you again. How did you get there? I couldn't believe my eyes, as the blind man said. Look at me. I'm not sure that you've grown prettier, but I like you all the same."

Margot suddenly gave a sob and turned away. He pulled her by the sleeve, but she turned away still farther. They revolved on one spot.

"For heaven's sake, say something. Where would you rather go—to my place or yours? What's the matter with you?"

She shook him off and walked quickly back to the corner. Rex followed her.

"What on earth is the matter with you?" he repeated in perplexity.

Margot hastened her steps. He caught her up again.

"Come along with me, you goose," said Rex. "Look, I've got something here . . ." He drew out his wallet.

Margot promptly struck him a backhand blow in the face.

"That ring on your forefinger is very sharp," he said calmly. And he continued to follow her, hurriedly fumbling in his wallet.

Margot ran to the entrance of the house and unlocked the door. Rex tried to thrust something into her hand, but suddenly he raised his eyes.

"Oh, that's the little game, is it?" he said, as he recognized the doorway from which they had just emerged.

Margot pushed open the door without looking round.

"Here, take it," he said roughly, and as she did not, he pushed it down inside her fur-collar. The door would have banged, had it not been of the reluctant, compressed-air kind. He stood there, pulled at his lower lip, and presently moved away.

Margot groped through the darkness up to the first landing, and was about to go on when suddenly she felt faint. She seated herself on a step and sobbed as she had never sobbed before—not even that time when he had left her. She felt something crinkly against her neck and grasped it. It was a piece of rough paper. She pressed the light-switch and saw that she was holding in her hand, not money, but a pencil drawing: the back view of a girl, bare-shouldered, bare-legged, on a bed, with her face to the wall. Under it a date was written, first in pencil, then overwritten in ink—the day, month and year when he had left her. That was why he had told her not to look round—because he was sketching her! Was it really only two years since that day?

The light went out with a thud, and Margot leaned against the grating of the lift crying afresh. She was crying because he had left her that time; because he had concealed his name and his reputation from her; because she might all this time have been happy with him if he had stayed; and because she would then have escaped the two Japanese, the old man and Albinus. And then she cried, too, because at supper Rex had touched her right knee and Albinus her left—as though _wow'_ Paradise had been on her right hand and Hell on her left.

She wiped her nose on her sleeve, groped in the darkness and pressed the switch again. The light calmed her a little. She examined the sketch once more; reflected that, however much it meant to her, it would be dangerous to keep it; tore it into fragments and flung these through the grating into the well of the lift. This reminded her of her early childhood. Then she pulled out her pocket mirror, powdered her face with a swift circular motion, straining her upper lip as she did so, closed her bag with a resolute click and ran up the steps.

"Why so late?" asked Albinus.

He was already in his pyjamas.

She explained breathlessly that she had found it difficult to get rid of von Ivanoff, who had kept insisting that she must let him drive her home.

"How my beauty's eyes are sparkling," he murmured, "and how tired and hot she is. My beauty has been drinking."

"No, leave me alone tonight," replied Margot softly.

"Bunny, please," implored Albinus, "I've been waiting so."

"Wait a bit longer. First I want to know some-

138

thing: have you done anything about the divorce yet?"

"The divorce?" he repeated, taken aback.

"Sometimes I can't understand you, Albert. After all, we must put things on a proper footing, mustn't we? Or perhaps you mean to leave me after a while and go back to Lizzy?"

"Leave you?"

"Stop repeating my words, you idiot. No, you shan't come near me till you give me a sensible answer."

"Very well," he said. "On Monday I'll speak to my lawyer."

"Positively? You promise?"

❧ 18 ❧

Axel Rex was glad to be back in his beautiful native land. He had been having troubles lately. Somehow, the hinges of luck had got stuck—and he had abandoned it in the mud like a broken car. There had been, for instance, that row with his editor who had failed to appreciate his last joke—not that it was ever intended for reproduction. There had been a row generally. A rich spinster had been mixed up in it and a fishy ("though very amusing," thought Rex sadly) money-transaction, and a rather one-sided conversation with certain authorities on the subject of undesirable aliens. People had been unkind to him, he reflected, but he forgave them readily. Funny the way people admired his work and the very next moment attempted (once or twice fairly successfully) to punch his face.

Worst of all, however, was the question of his financial position. Fame—not quite on the

140

world scale which that mild fool had yesterday suggested it to be—but still, fame—had brought in a good deal of money at one period. Now, when he was rather at a loose end and hazy about his cartoonist's career in Berlin, where people were, as they always had been, at the mother-in-law stage of humor, he would have had that money still—at least some of it—had he not been a gambler.

Having cultivated a penchant for bluff since his tenderest age, no wonder his favorite card-game was poker! He played it whenever he could get partners; and he played it in his dreams: with historical characters or some distant cousin of his, long dead, whom in real life he never remembered, or with people who—in real life again—would have flatly refused to be in the same room with him. In that dream he took up, stacked together, and lifted close to his eyes the five dealt to him, saw with pleasure the joker in cap and bells, and, as he pressed out with a cautious thumb one top corner and then another, he found by degrees that he had five jokers. "Excellent," he thought to himself, without any surprise at their plurality, and quietly made his first bet, which Henry the Eighth (by Holbein) who had only four queens, doubled. Then he woke up, still with his poker face.

The morning was so bleak and dark that he had to turn on his bedside light. The gauze on the window looked filthy. They could have given him a better room for his money (which, he thought, they might never see). Suddenly, with a sweet shock, he remembered that curious meeting yesterday.

As a rule, Rex recalled his love affairs without any particular emotion. Margot was an exception. In the course of these two last years, he had often found himself thinking of her; and he had often gazed with something very like melancholy at that rapid pencil sketch; a strange sentiment because Axel Rex was, to say the least of it, a cynic.

When, as a youth, he had first left Germany (very quickly, in order to avoid the War), he had abandoned his poor half-witted mother, and the day after his departure for Montevideo she had fallen downstairs and injured herself fatally. As a child he had poured oil over live mice, set fire to them and watched them dart about for a few seconds like flaming meteors. And it is best not to inquire into the things he did to cats. Then, in riper years, when his artistic talent developed, he tried in more subtle ways to satiate his curiosity, for it was not anything morbid with a medical name—oh, not at all—just cold, wide-eyed curiosity, just the marginal notes supplied by life to his art. It amused him immensely to see life made to look silly, as it slid helplessly into caricature. He despised practical jokes: he liked them to happen by themselves with perchance now and then just that little touch on his part which would send the wheel running downhill. He loved to fool people; and the less trouble the process entailed, the more the joke pleased him. And at the same time this dangerous man was, with pencil in hand, a very fine artist indeed.

Uncle alone in the house with the children said he'd dress up to amuse them. After a long wait, as he did not appear, they went down and saw a masked man putting the table silver into a bag. "Oh, Uncle," they cried in delight. "Yes, isn't my make-up good?" said Uncle, taking his mask off. Thus goes the Hegelian syllogism of humor. Thesis: Uncle made himself up as a burglar (a laugh for the children); antithesis: it was a burglar (a laugh for the reader); synthesis: it still was Uncle (fooling the reader). This was the super-humor Rex liked to put into his work; and this, he claimed, was quite new.

A great painter one day, high up on the scaffold, began moving backward to view better his finished fresco. The next receding step would have taken him over, and, as a warning cry might be fatal, his apprentice had the presence of mind to sling the contents of a pail at the masterpiece. Very funny! But how much funnier still, had the rapt master been left to walk back into nothing— with, incidentally, the spectators expecting the pail. (The art of caricature, as Rex understood it, was thus based (apart from its synthetic, fooled-again nature) on the contrast between cruelty on one side and credulity on the other. And if, in real life, Rex looked on without stirring a finger while a blind beggar, his stick tapping happily, was about to sit down on a freshly painted bench, he was only deriving inspiration for his next little picture.

But all this did not apply to the feelings which Margot had aroused in him. In her case, even in the artistic sense, the painter in Rex triumphed over the humorist. He felt a little annoyed at being so pleased to find her again: indeed, if he had left Margot, it had been only because he was afraid of becoming too fond of her.

Now first of all he wanted to find out whether she was really living with Albinus. He looked at his watch. Noon. He looked into his note-case. Empty. He dressed and made his way on foot to the house where he had been on the previous evening. Snow was falling softly and steadily.

Albinus happened to open the door himself and

did not at first recognize his guest in the snow-covered figure before him. But when Rex, after rubbing his shoes on the mat, raised his face, Albinus welcomed him very cordially. The man had impressed him the evening before not only by his ready wit and easy manner, but also by his extraordinary personal appearance: his pale, hollow cheeks, thick lips and queer black hair went to form a kind of fascinating ugliness. On the other hand it was pleasant to remember that Margot, when they were discussing the party, had observed: "That artist friend of yours has a revolting mug—there's a man I'd not kiss at any price." And what Dorianna had had to say of him was interesting too.

Rex apologized for the informality of his visit, and Albinus laughed genially.

"To tell the truth," Rex said, "you're one of the few people in Berlin whom I'd like to know more intimately. In America men make friends more easily than here and I've formed the habit over there of behaving unconventionally. Excuse me if I shock you—but do you really think it advisable to allow that natty rag-doll to straggle on your divan when there's a Ruysdael right above it? By the way, may I examine your pictures more closely? That one over there looks superb."

Albinus led him through the rooms. Every

one of them contained some fine painting—with a sprinkling of fakes. Rex gazed in rapture. He wondered whether that Lorenzo Lotto with the mauve-robed John and weeping Virgin was quite genuine. At one time of his adventurous life he had worked as a faker of pictures and had produced some very good stuff. The seventeenth century—that was his period. Last night he had noticed an old friend in the dining room, and now he examined it again with exquisite delight. It was in Baugin's best manner: a mandolin on a chessboard, ruby wine in a glass and a white carnation.

"Doesn't it look modern? Almost surrealistic, in fact," said Albinus fondly.

"Quite," said Rex, holding his own wrist, as he contemplated the picture. It was modern: he had painted it only eight years ago.

Then they walked along the passage where there was a nice Linard—flowers and an eyed moth. At that moment Margot emerged from the bathroom in a bright yellow bathrobe. She ran down the corridor, almost losing one of her slippers on the way.

"In here," said Albinus with a bashful laugh. Rex followed him into the library.

"If I am not mistaken," he said smiling, "that was Fräulein Peters. Is she a relative of yours?"

"What's the use of pretending?" thought Al-

146

binus swiftly. It would be impossible to hood-wink anyone so observant—and, well, wasn't it all rather smart—in a subtle Bohemian way? "My little mistress," he answered aloud.

He invited Rex to stay for dinner, and the latter made no ado about accepting. When Margot appeared at table, she was languid but calm: the agitation which she had been barely able to control the night before had now changed into something very like happiness. As she sat between these two men who were sharing her life, she felt as though she were the chief actress in a mysterious and passionate film-drama—so she tried to behave accordingly; smiling absently, drooping her eyelashes, tenderly laying her hand on Albinus' sleeve, as she asked him to pass the fruit, and casting a fleeting, indifferent glance at her former lover.

"No, I won't let him escape again, no fear," she said to herself suddenly, and a delicious, long-lost shudder ran down her spine.

Rex spoke a good deal. Among other amusing things he told them a funny story about an inebriated Lohengrin who happened to miss the swan and waited hopefully for the next one. Albinus laughed heartily, but Rex knew (and this was the private point of his joke) that he saw only half the joke, and that it was the other half which made Margot bite her lips. He hardly looked at her while talking. When he did, she at once cast a downward glance at this or that part of her dress where his eyes had settled for a moment, and touched it up unconsciously.

"And soon," said Albinus with a wink, "we'll be seeing someone on the screen."

Margot pouted and slapped his hand lightly.

"Are you an actress?" asked Rex. "Oh, indeed? And may I inquire in what film you are appearing?"

She answered without looking at him and felt extremely proud. He was a famous artist and she was a film star. They were now both on the same level.

Rex left immediately after dinner, reflected what he should do next and dropped into a gambling-club. A straight flush (which had not happened to him for ages) bucked him up somewhat. The next day he rang up Albinus and they went to an exhibition of pointedly modern pictures. The day after that, he had supper at Albinus' flat. Then he called unexpectedly, but Margot was not at home, and he had to sustain a good lengthy highbrow conversation with Albinus, who was beginning to like him hugely. Rex was getting thoroughly annoyed. At length fate took pity on him, choosing for her good deed the circumstance of an ice-hockey match at the Sport Palace.

As the three of them were making their way to their box, Albinus noticed Paul's shoulders and Irma's fair plait. Something of this kind was bound to happen one day or another, but although he had always been expecting it, it took him so entirely unawares that he veered awkwardly, bumping violently into Margot's side as he did so.

"Look what you're doing, you," she said nastily.

"Make yourself comfortable and order some coffee," said Albinus. "I must—er—telephone. I had quite forgotten."

"Please, don't go away," said Margot, standing up again.

"It's rather urgent," he insisted, hunching his shoulders, trying to make himself as small as possible (had Irma seen him?). "If I should be detained, don't worry. Do excuse me, Rex."

"Please, stay here," repeated Margot very quietly.

But he did not notice her strange glance, nor how her cheeks flushed and her lips quivered. His back became quite round, and he hurried to the exit.

There was a moment of silence and then Rex heaved a great sigh.

"*Enfin seuls*," he said grimly.

They sat side by side in their expensive box at a little table with a very white cloth. Below, just beyond the barrier, extended the vast frozen area. The band was playing a thumping circus march. The empty sheet of ice bore an oily blue gloss. The air was hot and cold at the same time.

"Do you understand now?" asked Margot suddenly, hardly knowing herself what she was asking.

Rex was about to answer, but at that moment a crash of applause reverberated through the enormous house. He squeezed her hot little fingers under the table. Margot felt the tears rising, but did not withdraw her hand.

A girl in white tights with a silvery, fluff-hemmed short skirt had come running across the ice on the toes of her skates and, having gained impetus, described a lovely curve and leaped, and turned, and was gliding again.

Her glittering skates flashed like lightning as she circled and danced, cutting the ice with an excruciating impact.

"You jilted me," Margot began.

"Yes, but I have dashed back to you, haven't I? Don't cry, baby. Have you been with him long?"

Margot tried to speak, but again a huge hubbub filled the house. The ice was empty again. She propped her elbows on the table and pressed her hands to her temples.

Among catcalls, clappings and clamor, the players were leisurely gliding across the ice—first the Swedes, then the Germans. The visitors' goal-keeper, in his brilliant sweater, with great leather pads from instep to hip, slid slowly toward his tiny goal.

"He's going to get her to divorce him. Do you understand what a very awkward moment you've chosen for coming?"

"Nonsense. Do you really believe he's going to marry you?"

"If you upset things he won't."

"No, Margot, he'll not marry you."

"And I tell you he will."

Their lips continued to move, but the clamor around drowned their swift quarrel. The crowd was roaring with excitement as nimble sticks pursued the puck on the ice, and knocked it, and hooked it, and passed it on, and missed it, and clashed together in rapid collision. Shifting smoothly this way and that at his post, the goal-keeper pressed his legs together so that his two pads combined to form one single shield.

". . . it's dreadful that you've come back.

You're a beggar compared with him. Good God, now I know you're going to spoil everything."

"Nonsense, nonsense, we'll be very careful."

"I'm going mad," said Margot. "Get me out of this din. Let's go. I'm sure he won't come back now, and if he does, it'll be a good lesson."

"Come to my place. You must come. Don't be a fool. We'll be quick. You'll be home in an hour."

"Shut up. I won't take any risks. I've been working to get him that far for months, and now he's ripe. Do you really expect me to throw it all up now?"

"He won't marry you," said Rex in a tone of conviction.

"Will you take me home or not?" she asked, almost screaming—and the thought flashed through her mind: "I'll let him kiss me in the taxi."

"Wait a bit. Say, how do you know I am broke?"

"I can see that in your eyes," she replied, and then stopped her ears, for now the noise had reached its climax: a goal had been scored, the Swedish goalkeeper was lying prone on the ice, and the stick which had been struck out of his hand spun round and round as it slid away on the ice like a lost oar.

"Well, what I say is this: it's a waste of time to put it off. It's got to happen sooner or later. Come on. There's a fine view from my window when the blind is down."

"Another word and I'll drive home alone."

As they were making their way along the back of the boxes, Margot gave a start and frowned. A plump gentleman in horn-rimmed glasses was staring at her with disgust. Seated by his side was a little girl following the game through a large pair of field glasses.

"Look round," snapped Margot to her companion, "do you see that fat bloke with the child? That's his brother-in-law and his daughter. Now I see why my worm crawled away. Pity I didn't notice them before. He was very rude to me once, so I wouldn't mind if somebody gave him a good hiding."

"And yet—you can talk of wedding bells," was Rex's comment as he walked down the soft wide steps by her side. "He'll never marry you. Now look here, my dear, I've got a new suggestion to make. And that's final, I guess."

"What's that?" asked Margot suspiciously.

"I'll take you home all right, but you'll have to pay for the cab, my dear."

⋈ 19 ⋉

PAUL gazed after her and the rolls of fat over his collar grew the color of beetroot. Despite the sweetness of his nature, he would not have minded doing to Margot what she suggested doing to him. He wondered who her companion might be, and where Albinus was; he felt sure that that gentleman must be somewhere about, and the thought that the child might suddenly see him was intolerable. He was much relieved when the whistle blew and he could escape with Irma.

They reached home. She looked tired, and in response to her mother's questions about the match only nodded, smiling that faint mysterious smile which was her most charming peculiarity.

"It's amazing the way they dash about on the ice," said Paul.

Elisabeth looked at him thoughtfully and then turned to her daughter. "Time for bed, time for bed," she said.

"Oh, no," entreated Irma sleepily.

"Goodness, it's nearly midnight, you've never been up so late."

"Tell me, Paul," said Elisabeth, when Irma was safely tucked up, "I've a feeling that something happened. I was so restless while you were away. Paul, tell me!"

"But I've nothing to tell," he said, growing very red in the face.

"You didn't meet anyone?" she ventured. "You really didn't?"

"What put such an idea into your head?" he muttered, thoroughly disconcerted by the almost telepathic sensibility which Elisabeth had developed since the separation from her husband.

"I'm always fearing it," she whispered, slowly bending her head.

The next morning Elisabeth was roused by the nurse who came into the room with a thermometer in her hand.

"Irma's ill, ma'am," she said briskly. "Her temperature is up to a hundred and one."

"A hundred and one," echoed Elisabeth, and she suddenly thought: "That's why I was so uneasy yesterday."

She sprang out of bed and flew into the nursery. Irma was lying on her back, staring up at the ceiling with glistening eyes.

"A fisherman and a boat," she said, pointing up at the ceiling on which the rays of the bedside lamp cast a sort of pattern. It was quite early and snowing.

"Does your throat hurt, my pet?" asked Elisabeth, still struggling with her dressing-gown. Then she bent anxiously over the child's pointed little face.

"My God, how hot her forehead is!" she exclaimed, stroking back the fine pale hair from Irma's brow.

"And one, two, three, four reeds," said Irma softly, still looking up.

"We'd better ring up the doctor," said Elisabeth.

"Oh, there's no need for that, ma'am," said the nurse. "I'll give her some hot tea with lemon and a nice aspirin. Everybody's got the 'flu now."

Elisabeth knocked at Paul's door. He was shaving and with the lather still on his cheeks he went to Irma's room. Paul often cut himself when he shaved, even with the safety razor—and now a bright red patch was spreading through the froth on his chin.

"Strawberries and whipped cream," said Irma softly as he bent over her.

The doctor arrived toward evening, seated him-

156

self on the edge of Irma's bed and, with his eyes fixed on a corner of the room, began to count her pulse-beats. Irma gazed at the white hair in the cavity of his large complicated ear and at the W-shaped vein on his pink temple.

"Good," said the doctor, looking at her over the rim of his spectacles. Then he told Irma to sit up and Elisabeth drew up the child's nightdress. Irma's body was very white and thin, with prominent shoulder blades. The doctor put his stethoscope to her back, breathing heavily, and told her to breathe too.

"Good," he said again.

Then he tapped her on different parts of the chest and ploughed her stomach with icy-cold fingers. At last he stood up, patted her head, washed his hands, turned down his cuffs, and Elisabeth led him into the study, where he sat down comfortably, unscrewed his fountain pen and wrote out his prescriptions.

"Yes," he said, "there's a lot of influenza about. Yesterday a recital had to be canceled because the singer and her accompanist were both down with it."

Next morning Irma's temperature was considerably lower. Paul, on the other hand, was very seedy; he wheezed and kept blowing his nose but flatly refused to take to his bed and even went to his office as usual. The Fräulein, too, was sniffling.

That evening when Elisabeth drew out the warm glass tube from under her daughter's arm, she was delighted to see that the mercury had hardly risen above the red fever line. Irma blinked, the light dazzled her; and presently she turned her face to the wall. The room grew dark again. All was warm, cosy and a little absurd. Soon Irma fell asleep, but she woke up in the middle of the night from a vaguely unpleasant dream. She was thirsty and she felt for the sticky glass of lemonade which was on the bed table, emptied it and carefully set it back again, smacking her lips gently.

The room seemed to her darker than usual. In the next room the nurse was snoring violently, almost ecstatically. Irma listened to her, and then she began to wait for the friendly rumble of the electric train which emerged from underground very near the house. But it did not come. Perhaps it was too late, and the trains had stopped running. Irma lay with wide-opened eyes. Suddenly she heard from the street a familiar whistle on four notes. That was exactly how her father whistled, when he used to come home—just to let them know that he would be with them in a moment and that supper could be served. Irma knew perfectly well that it was not he, but a man who had for the last fortnight been visiting the lady on the fourth floor—the porter's little daughter had told her as much, and had put out her tongue when Irma observed, very reasonably, that it was stupid to come so late. She knew, too, that she must not talk about her father who was living with his little friend: this Irma had gathered from the conversation of two ladies who were walking downstairs in front of her.

The whistle beneath the window was repeated. Irma thought: "Who knows? Perhaps it *is* father after all? And no one will let him in; perhaps they told me on purpose that it was a strange man?"

She threw off the bedclothes and went on tiptoe to the window. As she did so, she knocked against a chair and something soft (her elephant) fell with a thud and a squeak; but Fräulein snored on unconcernedly. She opened the window and a delicious ice-cold gust of air entered the room. In the street, in darkness, somebody was standing, gazing up at the house. She looked down at him for quite a long time, but to her great disappointment it was not her father. The man stood

159

and stood. Then he turned round and walked away slowly. Irma felt sorry for him. She was so numb with cold that she could scarcely shut the window, and could not get warm again when she went back to her bed. At length she fell asleep and dreamed that she was playing hockey with her father. He laughed, slipped and fell on his bottom, losing his top hat, and she bumped down too. The ice was awful, but she could not get up and her hockey stick walked away like a looping caterpillar.

The next morning her temperature was up to a hundred and four, her face livid, and she complained of a pain in her side. The doctor was summoned immediately.

The patient's pulse was a hundred and twenty, the chest over the seat of the pain was dull on percussion and the stethoscope revealed fine crepitation. He ordered blistering, phenacetin and a soothing medicine. Elisabeth felt suddenly that she would go out of her mind, that, after all that had happened, fate simply had not the right to torture her like this. With a great effort she pulled herself together as she said good-by to the doctor. Before leaving he had a look at the nurse, who was in a high fever, but in the case of this vigorous woman there was no cause for alarm.

Paul accompanied him to the hall and asked in a hoarse voice—he was trying to whisper through his cold—whether there was any danger.

"I'll look in again today," answered the doctor slowly.

"Always the same," thought old Lampert, as he went downstairs. "Always the same questions, the same imploring glances." He consulted his notebook and slipped behind the steering wheel of his car, slamming the door as he did so. Five minutes later he was entering another house.

Albinus received him in the silk-braided warm jacket which he put on when at work in his study.

"She hasn't been feeling very well since yesterday," he said worriedly. "She complains that she aches all over."

"Temperature?" asked Lampert, wondering whether he should tell this anxious lover that his daughter had pneumonia.

"No, that's just it: she doesn't seem to have a temperature," said Albinus in a tone of alarm. "And I was told that influenza *without* feverish symptoms is particularly dangerous."

("Why should I tell him?" thought Lampert. "He deserted his family without a qualm. They'll tell him themselves if they want to. Why should I interfere?")

"Well," said Lampert with a sigh, "let's have a look at our charming invalid."

Margot was lying on the sofa, cross and flushed, enveloped in a silk wrapper with a great deal of lace. Beside her sat Rex with his legs crossed, sketching her lovely head on the bottom of a cigarette box.

("A lovely creature, unquestionably," thought Lampert, "but there *is* something snakelike about her.")

Rex retired into the next room, whistling. Albinus hovered close at hand. Lampert proceeded to examine the patient. A slight chill, that was all.

"You'd better stay indoors for two or three days," said Lampert. "How's the film going, by the way? Finished?"

"Yes, thank God," answered Margot, drawing her wrap round her languidly. "And next month there's to be a private view of it. I must be well by that time, whatever happens."

("And moreover," reflected Lampert irrelevantly, "this little slut is going to be the ruin of him.")

When the doctor had gone, Rex returned to Margot's side and went on sketching idly, whistling through his teeth all the time. For some moments Albinus stood near him, his head cocked, following the rhythmic movements of

162

that bony white hand. Then he went off to his study to finish an article about a much-discussed exhibition.

"Rather nice, being the friend of the house," said Rex with a snort of laughter.

Margot looked at him and said angrily:

"Yes, I do love you, ugly—but there's nothing doing, you know that yourself."

He twisted the cigarette box round and then sent it spinning onto the table.

"Listen, my dear, you've got to come to me some day, that's plain. My visits here are very exhilarating, of course, and all that, but I'm getting sick of this kind of fun."

"In the first place—please don't shout. You won't be satisfied until we've done something idiotically rash. At the least provocation, at the least suspicion, he'll kill me or turn me out of the house, and we shall neither of us have a penny."

"Kill you," chuckled Rex, "that's rich."

"Do, please, wait a little. Don't you understand? Once he has married me, I shall be less nervous and freer to act as I choose. A wife can't be got rid of so easily. Besides, there's the film. I've all sorts of plans."

"The film," laughed Rex again.

"Yes, you'll see. I'm certain it's going to be a

great hit. We must wait. I'm just as impatient as you are, my love."

He seated himself on the edge of her sofa and laid his arm round her shoulder.

"No, no," she said, shivering and half-closing her eyes already.

"Just one tiny little kiss."

"Very tiny," she said in a smothered voice.

He bent over her, but suddenly a door clicked in the distance and they heard Albinus approaching: carpet, floor, carpet, floor again.

Rex was about to raise himself, but at the same moment he noticed that a button of his coat was caught in the lace on Margot's shoulder. Margot tried to disentangle it swiftly. Rex tugged, but the lace refused to give way. Margot grunted in dismay, as she pulled at the knot with her sharp shiny nails. At that moment Albinus swept into the room.

"No, I'm not embracing Fräulein Peters," said Rex coolly. "I was only making her comfortable and got entangled, you see."

Margot was still worrying the lace without raising her lashes. The situation was farcical in the extreme and Rex was enjoying it hugely.

Albinus silently drew out a fat penknife with a dozen blades and opened what turned out to be

164

a small file. He tried again and broke his nail. The burlesque was developing nicely.

"For heaven's sake, don't stab her," said Rex ecstatically.

"Hands off," said Albinus—but Margot screamed:

"Don't you dare cut the lace; cut off the button!"

"Stop—it's my button!" yelled Rex.

For a moment it looked as if both men were falling on top of her. Rex gave a final tug, something snapped, and he was free.

"Come to my study," said Albinus to him darkly.

"Now let's be smart," thought Rex; and he recalled a dodge which had helped him once before to fool a rival.

"Please, sit down," said Albinus with a heavy frown. "What I want to tell you is rather important. It's about this White Raven exhibition. I was wondering whether you'd care to help me. You see, I'm just finishing a rather involved and—well—subtle article, and several exhibitors are receiving rather rough treatment at my hands."

("Oho!" thought Rex. "So that's why you looked so lugubrious. Gloom of the learned mind? Throes of inspiration? Gorgeous.")

165

"Now, what I'd like you to do," Albinus went on, "is to illustrate my article by throwing in little caricatures—stressing the things I criticize, lampooning both color and line—as you once did with Barcelo."

"I'm your man," said Rex. "But I, too, have a little request. You know what I mean—expecting various fees and being rather short of ready money. Could you make me an advance? Just a trifle—five hundred marks, shall we say."

"Why, of course. More, if you like. Anyway, you must fix the fee for the drawings."

"Is this a catalogue?" asked Rex. "May I have a look at it? Girls, girls, girls," he continued with marked disgust, as he considered the reproductions. "Square girls, slanting girls, girls with elephantiasis . . ."

"And why, pray," asked Albinus slyly, "do girls bore you so?"

Rex explained quite frankly.

"Well, that's only a matter of taste, I suppose," said Albinus, who prided himself on his broad-mindedness. "Of course, I don't condemn you. It's a thing widely spread, I believe, among men of artistic temperament. In a shopkeeper, it would repel me, but in a painter, it's quite different—quite likeable, in fact, and romantic—romance coming from Rome. Nevertheless," he

166

added, "I can assure you that you lose a great deal."

"No, thank you. A woman for me is only a harmless mammal, or a jolly companion—sometimes."

Albinus laughed. "Well, as you are so outspoken about it, let me, in my turn, confess something to you. That actress woman, Karenina, said as soon as she saw you that she was sure you were indifferent to the gentler sex."

("Oh, did she?" thought Rex.)

❧ 20 ❧

A few days passed. Margot still had a cough and, as she was apt to get very nervous about herself, she stayed at home, and for lack of something to do—reading not being her forte—she amused herself in the way Rex had recommended: lying comfortably in a bright chaos of cushions, she consulted the telephone book and rang up unknown individuals, shops and business firms. She ordered prams, and lilies, and radio sets to be sent to addresses selected at random; she made fools of worthy citizens and advised their wives to be less credulous; she rang up the same number ten times in succession, thereby reducing Messrs. Traum, Baum & Käsebier to desperation. She received wonderful declarations of love and still more wonderful curses. Albinus came in and stood watching her with a fond smile while she ordered a coffin for a certain Frau Kirchhof. Her kimono was undone, the little feet were kicking in malicious delight, the long eyes moved to and fro, as she listened. Albinus was filled with a passionate tenderness, and he quietly stood a little way off, afraid to approach, afraid of spoiling her pleasure.

Now she was telling Professor Grimm the story of her life, and imploring him to meet her at midnight, while, at the other end of the wire, the Professor was painfully and ponderously debating with himself whether this invitation was a hoax or the result of his fame as an ichthyologist.

In view of Margot's telephonic frolics it was not surprising that Paul had been vainly trying to get through to Albinus for the last half hour. He kept ringing up and every time was met by the same remorseless buzz.

At last he rose, felt a rush of giddiness and heavily sat down again. He had not slept for two nights; he was sick and in a storm of grief; but all the same he had to do it, and it was going to be done. The persistent buzz seemed to mean that fate was determined to thwart his intention, but Paul was stubborn: if he could not do it this way he would try another.

He tiptoed into the nursery which was dark and—despite the presence of several persons—very quiet. He saw the back of his sister's head, the comb behind and the woolen shawl round her shoulders; and suddenly he turned round resolutely, stepped out into the hall, dragged on his overcoat (groaning and choking down his sobs) and set off to fetch Albinus.

"Wait," he said to the taxi driver as he alighted on the pavement before the familiar house.

He was already pushing the entrance door when Rex hurried up from behind. Both men entered at the same moment. They looked at one another and—there was a great outburst of cheering as the puck was shot into the Swedish goal.

"Are you on your way to see Herr Albinus?" asked Paul grimly.

Rex smiled and nodded his head.

"Then let me tell you that he won't be receiving any visitors just now. I'm his wife's brother and have some very bad news for him."

"Would you like to entrust me with your message?" inquired Rex blandly.

Paul suffered from shortness of breath. He halted on the first landing. With lowered head, like a bull, he gazed at Rex, who looked back curiously and expectantly at his puffed-up, tear-stained face.

"I advise you to postpone your visit," said Paul, breathing heavily. "My brother-in-law's little girl is dying." He continued his way up the stairs and Rex followed him quietly.

Hearing the impertinent steps behind him, Paul felt the blood rush to his head, but was afraid of being delayed by his asthma, and so controlled himself. When they reached the door of the flat he again turned to Rex and said:

"I don't know who and what you are, but I'm at a loss to understand your persistence."

"Oh, my name is Axel Rex and I'm quite at home here," replied Rex affably, as he stretched out a long, white finger and pressed the electric bell.

"Shall I hit him?" thought Paul, and then: "What does it matter now? . . . The main thing is to get it over quickly."

A short, gray-haired footman (the English lord had been sacked) let them in.

"Tell your master," said Rex with a sigh, "that this gentleman here would like—"

"Shut up, you!" said Paul, and, standing in the middle of the hall, he shouted as loudly as he could: "Albert!" and again: "Albert!"

When Albinus saw the distorted face of his brother-in-law, he made an awkward little rush toward him, skidded and then came to a dead stop.

"Irma is dangerously ill," said Paul, thumping

171

with his stick on the floor. "You'd better come at once."

A brief silence ensued. Rex surveyed them both greedily. Suddenly Margot's shrill voice rang out from the drawing room: "Albert, I've got to speak to you."

"Just coming," stammered Albinus, and he hurried into the drawing room. Margot was standing with her arms crossed on her breast.

"My little girl is dangerously ill," said Albinus. "I'm going to see her at once."

"They are lying to you," Margot cried angrily. "It's a trap to entice you back."

"Margot . . . for God's sake!"

She seized his hand: "And what if I come with you?"

"Margot, enough! You must understand . . . Where's my lighter? Where's my lighter? Where's my lighter? He's waiting for me."

"They're fooling you. I won't let you go."

"They're waiting for me," Albinus stammered out with wide-open eyes.

"If you dare—"

Paul was standing in the hall, in the same posture, prodding the floor with his stick. Rex produced a tiny enamel box. From the drawing room came the blare of excited voices. Rex offered Paul some cough-drops. Paul pushed back with his

elbow without looking and spilled the sweets.
Rex laughed. Again—that outburst of voices.

"Ghastly," murmured Paul and walked out.
With his cheeks quivering, he hurried downstairs.

"Well?" asked Fräulein in a whisper when he
got back.

"No, he's not coming," answered Paul. He covered his eyes with his hand for a moment, cleared
his throat, and, as before, tiptoed into the nursery.

Nothing had changed there. Softly, rhyth-
mically, Irma was tossing her head to and fro
on the pillow. Her half-opened eyes were dim;
every now and then a hiccough shook her. Elisabeth smoothed the bedclothes: a mechanical gesture devoid of sense. A spoon fell off the table,
and its delicate jingle lingered for a long time in
the ears of those in the room. The hospital nurse
counted the pulse-beats, blinked, and cautiously,
as though afraid of hurting it, put back the little
hand on the coverlet.

"She's thirsty, perhaps?" whispered Elisabeth.

The nurse shook her head. Someone in the
room coughed very softly. Irma tossed about;
then she raised one slight knee under the bedclothes and presently stretched it out again very
slowly.

A door creaked, Fräulein came in and said
something in Paul's ear. Paul nodded and she

went out. Presently the door creaked again; but Elisabeth did not turn her head . . .

The man who had entered halted a couple of feet from the bed. He could only dimly discern his wife's fair hair and shawl, but with agonizing distinctness he saw Irma's face—her small, black nostrils and the yellowish gloss of her rounded forehead. He stood like this for a long time, then he opened his mouth very wide and somebody (a distant cousin of his) seized him under the armpits from behind.

He found himself sitting in Paul's study. On the divan in the corner two ladies, whose names he could not remember, were seated, talking in low tones; he had a queer feeling that if he remembered, everything would be right again. Huddled in an armchair, Irma's Fräulein was sobbing. A dignified old gentleman with a great, bald brow was standing at the window smoking, and every now and then lifting himself from heel to toe. On the table, a glass bowl with oranges gleamed.

"Why didn't they send for me before?" muttered Albinus, raising his eyebrows, without addressing anybody in particular. He frowned, shook his head and cracked his finger-joints. Silence. The clock on the mantelpiece ticked. Lampert came in from the nursery.

"Well?" asked Albinus hoarsely.

Lampert turned to the dignified old gentleman, who shrugged his shoulders slightly and followed him into the sickroom.

A long time elapsed. The windows were quite dark; nobody had troubled to draw the curtains. Albinus took an orange and began peeling it slowly. Outside, snow was falling, and only muffled noises rose from the street. From time to time a tinkling sound came from the central heating apparatus. Down in the street someone whistled four notes (Siegfried); and then all was silent again. Albinus slowly ate the orange. It was very sour. Suddenly Paul came into the room, and without looking at anyone uttered a single short word.

In the nursery, Albinus saw his wife's back, as she bent, motionless and intent, over the bed, still holding, it seemed, a ghostly glass in her hand. The hospital nurse put her arm round her shoulders and led her into dimness. Albinus walked up to the bed. For a moment he had a vague glimpse of a little dead face and of a short pale lip with bared front teeth—and one little milk-tooth was missing. Then all became misty before his eyes. He turned round and very carefully, trying not to jostle against anybody or anything, went out. The front-door below was locked.

But as he stood there, a painted lady in a Spanish shawl came down, opened it and let in a snow-covered man. Albinus looked at his watch. It was past midnight. Had he really been there five hours?

He walked along the white, soft, crunching pavement, and still could not quite believe what had happened. In his mind's eye he pictured Irma with surprising vividness, scrambling onto Paul's knees or patting a light ball against the wall with her hands; but the taxis hooted as if nothing had happened, the snow glittered Christmas-like under the lamps, the sky was black, and only in the distance, beyond the dark mass of roofs, in the direction of the Gedächtniskirche, where the great picture-palaces were, did the blackness melt to a warm brownish blush. All at once he remembered the names of the two ladies on the divan: Blanche and Rosa von Nacht.

At length he reached home. Margot was lying supine, smoking lustily. Albinus was vaguely aware of having quarreled with her hideously, but that did not matter now. She followed his movements in silence, as he quietly walked up and down the room and wiped his face, which was wet from the snow. All she felt now was delicious content. Rex had left a short time before, well-contented too.

ৼ 21 ৼ

PERHAPS for the first time in the course of the year he had spent with Margot, Albinus was perfectly conscious of the thin, slimy layer of turpitude which had settled on his life. Now, with dazzling distinctness, fate seemed to be urging him to come to his senses; he heard her thunderous summons; he realized what a rare opportunity was being offered him to raise his life to its former level; and he knew, with the lucidity of grief, that if he returned to his wife now, the reconciliation, which under ordinary circumstances would have been impossible, would come about almost of itself.

Certain recollections of that night gave him no peace: he remembered how Paul had suddenly glanced at him with a moist imploring look, and then, turning away, had squeezed his arm slightly. He remembered how, in the mirror, he had had a fleeting glimpse of his wife's eyes, in which there had been a heart-rending expression—pitiful, hunted—but still akin to a smile.

He pondered over all this with deep emotion. Yes—if he were to go to his little girl's funeral, he would stay with his wife forever.

He rang up Paul and the maid told him the place and hour of the burial. Next morning he rose, while Margot was still asleep, and ordered the servant to get him his black coat and top hat. After he had hastily swallowed some coffee, he went into Irma's former nursery—where a long table, with a green net across it, now stood; listlessly he took up a small celluloid ball and let it bounce, but instead of thinking of his child he saw another figure, a graceful, lively, wanton girl, laughing, leaning over the table, one heel raised, as she thrust out her ping-pong bat.

It was time to start. In a few minutes he would be holding Elisabeth under the elbow, in front of an open grave. He threw the little ball on the table and went quickly into the bedroom, in order to see Margot asleep for the last time. And, as he stood by the bed and feasted his eyes on that childish face, with the soft pink lips and flushed cheeks, Albinus remembered their first night together and thought with horror of his future by the side of his pale, faded wife. This future seemed to him like one of those long, dim, dusty passages where one finds a nailed-up box—or an empty perambulator.

With an effort, he turned his eyes away from the sleeping girl, nervously bit his thumbnail and walked to the window. It was thawing. Bright motorcars were splashing their way through the puddles; at the corner a ragged rapscallion was selling violets; an adventurous Alsatian was insistently following a tiny Pekinese, which snarled, turned and slithered at the end of its leash; a great brilliant slice of the rapid blue sky was mirrored in a glass pane which a bare-armed servant girl was washing vigorously.

"Why are you up so early? Where are you going?" asked Margot in a drawling voice broken by a yawn.

"Nowhere," he said, without turning round.

ᥱ§ 22 ᥲᵉ

"Don't be so depressed, woggy," she said to him a fortnight later. "I know that it's all very sad, but they've grown to be almost strangers to you; you feel that yourself, don't you? And of course, they turned the little girl against you. Believe me, I do quite enter into your feelings, although if I could have a child, I'd rather have a boy."

"You're a child yourself," said Albinus, stroking her hair.

"Today of all days we must be in good spirits," continued Margot. "Today of all days! It's the beginning of my career. I'll be famous."

"Why yes, I had forgotten. When is it? Really today?"

Rex sauntered in. Of late, he had been with them every day, and Albinus had poured out his heart to him on several occasions and told him all that he could not say to Margot. Rex listened so kindly, made such sensible comments and was so sympathetic that the shortness of their acquaintance seemed to Albinus a mere accident in no way connected with the inner, spiritual time during which their friendship had developed and matured.

"One can't build up one's life on the quicksands of misfortune," Rex had said to him. "That is a sin against life. I once had a friend who was a sculptor and whose unerring appreciation of form was almost uncanny. Then, all of a sudden, out of pity he married an ugly, elderly hunchback. I don't know exactly what happened, but one day, soon after their marriage, they packed two little suitcases, one for each, and went on foot to the nearest lunatic asylum. In my opinion, an artist must let himself be guided solely by his sense of beauty: that will never deceive him."

"Death," he had said on another occasion, "seems to be merely a bad habit, which nature is at present powerless to overcome. I once had a dear friend—a beautiful boy full of life, with the face of an angel and the muscles of a panther. He cut himself while opening a tin of preserved peaches—you know, the large, soft, slippery kind that plap in the mouth and slither down. He died a few days later of blood poisoning. Fatuous, isn't it? And yet . . . yes, it is strange, but true, that, viewed as a work of art, the shape of his life would not have been so perfect had he been left to grow old. Death often is the point of life's joke."

On such occasions Rex could talk endlessly, indefatigably, inventing stories about non-existent friends and propounding reflections not too profound for the mind of his listener and couched in a sham-brilliant form. His culture was patchy, but his mind shrewd and penetrating, and his itch to make fools of his fellow men amounted almost to genius. Perhaps the only real thing about him was his innate conviction that everything that had ever been created in the domain of art, science or sentiment, was only a more or less clever trick. No matter how important the subject under discussion, he could always find something witty or trite to say about it, supplying exactly what his listener's mind or mood demanded, though, at the same time, he could be impossibly rude and overbearing when his interlocutor annoyed him. Even when he was talking quite seriously about a book or a picture, Rex had a pleasant feeling that he was a partner in a conspiracy, the partner of some ingenious quack—namely, the author of the book or the painter of the picture.

He watched with interest the sufferings of Albinus (in his opinion an oaf with simple passions

and a solid, too solid, knowlege of painting) , who
thought, poor man, that he had touched the very
depths of human distress; whereas Rex reflected—
with a sense of pleasant anticipation—that, far
from being the limit, it was merely the first item
in the program of a roaring comedy at which he,
Rex, had been reserved a place in the stage manager's private box. The stage manager of this
performance was neither God nor the devil. The
former was far too gray, and venerable, and old-
fashioned; and the latter, surfeited with other
people's sins, was a bore to himself and to others,
as dull as rain . . . in fact, rain at dawn in the
prison-court, where some poor imbecile, yawning
nervously, is being quietly put to death for the
murder of his grandmother. The stage manager
whom Rex had in view was an elusive, double,
triple, self-reflecting magic Proteus of a phan-
tom, the shadow of many-colored glass balls flying in a curve, the ghost of a juggler on a shimmering curtain. . . . This, at any rate, was what
Rex surmised in his rare moments of philosophic
meditation.

He took life lightly, and the only human
feeling that he ever experienced was his keen
liking for Margot, which he endeavored to explain
to himself by her physical characteristics, by
something in the odor of her skin, the epithelium

of her lips, the temperature of her body. But this was not quite the true explanation. Their mutual passion was based on a profound affinity of souls, though Margot was a vulgar little Berlin girl and he—a cosmopolitan artist.

When Rex called, on that day of all days, he managed to tell her, as he was helping her on with her coat, that he had rented a room where they could meet undisturbed. She flung him an angry glance—for Albinus was patting his pockets only ten paces away. Rex chuckled and added, hardly lowering his voice, that he would expect her there every day at a given hour.

"I'm inviting Margot to a rendezvous, but she won't come," he brightly said to Albinus as they were walking downstairs.

"Let her just try," smiled Albinus, pinching Margot's cheek affectionately. "Now we shall see what sort of an actress you are," he added, drawing on his gloves.

"Tomorrow at five, Margot, eh?" said Rex.

"Tomorrow the child is going to choose herself a car," said Albinus, "so she can't come to you."

"She'll have plenty of time in the morning for choosing. Does five suit you, Margot? Or shall we say six and clinch it?"

184

Margot suddenly lost her temper. "Idiotic joke," she said through her teeth.

The two men laughed and exchanged amused glances.

The hall-porter who was talking to the postman outside gazed at them curiously as they passed.

"It's hardly believable," said he when they were out of hearing, "that that Herr's little daughter died a couple of weeks ago."

"And who's the other Herr?" asked the postman.

"Don't ask *me*. An additional lover, I suppose. To tell the truth, I'm ashamed that the other tenants should see it all. And yet he's a rich, generous gentleman. What I always say is: if he's got to have a mistress, he might have chosen a larger and plumper one."

"Love is blind," remarked the postman thoughtfully.

~§ 23 §~

IN THE little hall where the film was to be viewed by a score of actors and guests, Margot felt a blissful shudder run down her back. Not far away she noticed the film manager in whose office she had once been made to feel so ridiculous. He walked up to Albinus, and Albinus introduced him to Margot. He had a large yellow stye on his right eyelid.

Margot was vexed that he did not recognize her.

"We had a talk a couple of years ago," she said slyly.

"Quite right," he replied with a polite smile. "I remember you perfectly." (He did not.)

As soon as the lights were out, Rex, who was seated between Margot and Albinus, fumbled for her hand and clasped it. In front of them, Dorianna Karenina was sitting in her sumptuous fur

186

coat, although the room was hot, between the producer and the film-man with the stye, to whom she was trying to be very nice.

The title, and then the names, unrolled with a diffident quiver. The apparatus hummed softly and monotonously, rather like a distant vacuum cleaner. There was no music.

Margot appeared on the screen almost at once. She was reading a book; then she slapped it down and lurched to the window; her fiancé was riding past.

Margot was so horrified that she wrenched her hand away from Rex. Who on earth was that ghastly creature? Awkward and ugly, with a swollen, strangely altered, leech-black mouth, misplaced brows and unexpected creases in her dress, the girl on the screen stared wildly in front of her and then broke in two with her stomach on the window sill and her buttocks to the spectators. Margot thrust away Rex's groping hand. She wanted to bite someone, or to throw herself on the floor and kick.

That monster on the screen had nothing in common with her—she was awful, awful! She was in fact like her mother, the porter's wife, in her wedding photograph.

"Perhaps it'll be better later on," she thought miserably.

Albinus bent over to her, almost embracing Rex, as he did so, and whispered tenderly:

"Sweet, marvelous, I had no idea . . ."

He really was enchanted: somehow he recalled the little "Argus" cinema where they had first met, and it touched him that Margot should act so atrociously—and yet with such a delightful childish zeal, like a schoolgirl reciting a birthday poem.

Rex was delighted too. He had never doubted that Margot would be a failure on the screen, and he knew that she would revenge herself on Albinus for this failure. Tomorrow, by way of reaction, she would come. At five punctually. It was all very pleasant. His hand went groping once more, and suddenly she gave him a violent pinch.

After a short absence Margot reappeared: she stole furtively along house-fronts, patting the walls and looking over her shoulder (although, queerly enough, causing not the slightest surprise to the passers-by) and then crept into a café where a good soul had told her she might find her lover in the company of a vamp (Dorianna Karenina). She crept in, and her back looked fat and clumsy.

"I shall yell in a moment," thought Margot.

Fortunately, there came a timely fade-in, and there was disclosed a little table in the café, a bottle in an ice-pail and the hero offering Dori-

anna a cigarette, then lighting it for her (which
gesture, in every producer's mind, is the symbol
of newborn intimacy). Dorianna threw back her
head, breathed out the smoke and smiled with
one corner of her mouth.

Someone in the hall began to clap; others
joined in. Then Margot appeared, the applause
was hushed. Margot opened her mouth, as in
real life she never opened it, and then, with
drooping head and dangling arms, came out into
the street again.

Dorianna, the real Dorianna, who was sitting
in front of them, turned round and her eyes
beamed amiably in the semi-darkness: "Bravo,
little girl," she said in her husky voice, and Margot would have liked to scratch her face.

Now she so dreaded her every re-appearance on
the screen that she felt quite faint and was no
longer capable of pushing and pinching Rex's persistent hand. He felt her hot breath in his ear,
as she moaned gently: "Please, stop, or I'll change
my seat." He patted her knee and withdrew his
hand.

The forsaken sweetheart returned and her
every movement was agony to Margot. She felt
like a soul in Hell to whom the demons are dis-
playing the unsuspected lining of its earthly trans-
gressions. Those stiff, clumsy, angular gestures

. . . In her bloated face she somehow recognized her mother's expression when the latter was trying to be polite to an influential tenant.

"A most successful scene," whispered Albinus, bending over to her again.

Rex was getting bored with sitting in the dark, watching a bad film and having a large man lean over him. He closed his eyes, saw the little colored caricatures he had been doing lately for Albinus, and meditated over the fascinating though quite simple problem of how to suck some more cash out of him.

The drama was drawing to a close. The hero, deserted by the vamp, made his way to a chemist's, in a good cinematic downpour, to buy himself some poison, but remembered his old mother and went back to his native farm instead. There, among hens and pigs, his original sweetheart was playing with their illegitimate baby (it would not remain illegitimate long now, judging by the way he peered over the fence). This was Margot's best scene. But, as the infant snuggled up to her, she suddenly stroked down her dress with the back of her hand (quite unintentionally) as if she were wiping her hand—and the infant gazed at her askance. A laugh rippled through the hall. Margot could stand it no longer and began to cry softly.

As soon as the lights went up, she left her seat and walked rapidly toward the exit.

With a worried look of apprehension, Albinus hurried after her.

Rex got up and stretched himself. Dorianna touched his arm. Beside her stood the man with the stye, yawning.

"A failure," said Dorianna, winking. "Poor little lass."

"And are you satisfied with your performance?" asked Rex curiously.

Dorianna laughed. "I'll tell you a secret: a true actress cannot be satisfied."

"Nor can the public sometimes," said Rex calmly. "By the way, do tell me, my dear, how did you come to hit on your stage name? It sort of disturbs me."

"Oh, that's a long story," she answered wistfully. "If you come to tea with me one day, I shall perhaps tell you more about it. The boy who suggested this name committed suicide."

"Ah—and no wonder. But what I wanted to know . . . Tell me, have you read Tolstoy?"

"Doll's Toy?" queried Dorianna Karenina. "No, I'm afraid not. Why?"

❦ 24 ❧

THERE were stormy scenes at home, sobs, moans, hysterics. She flung herself on the sofa, the bed, the floor. Her eyes sparkled brilliantly and wrathfully; one of her stockings had slipped down. The world was swamped in tears.

Albinus, as he tried to console her, unconsciously used the very words with which he had once comforted Irma when he kissed a bruise—words which now, after Irma's death, were vacant.

At first Margot vented her whole wrath upon him; then she abused Dorianna in terrible language; after which she assailed the producer. On the way she had a fling at Grossman, the old man with the stye, though he had had nothing at all to do with the matter.

"All right," said Albinus at last. "I'll do everything I possibly can for you. But I really don't think it was a failure. On the contrary, in several of the scenes you acted very well—in that first one, for instance, you know, when you—"

"Hold your tongue!" shrieked Margot, flinging an orange at him.

"But do listen to me, my pet. I'm prepared to do anything to make my darling happy. Now let's take a fresh handkerchief and dry up our tears for good. I'll tell you what I'll do. The film belongs to me. I've paid for the rubbish—I mean the rubbish Schwarz has made of it. I shall refuse to allow it to be shown anywhere, and I'll keep it as a souvenir for myself."

"No, burn it," sobbed Margot.

"Very well, I'll burn it. Dorianna won't be overpleased with that, I can assure you. Now—are we satisfied?"

She still went on sobbing, but more quietly.

"Come, come, don't cry any more, darling. To-morrow you shall go and choose yourself something. Shall I tell you what? A big thing on four wheels. Have you forgotten that? Now, won't that be fun? Then you'll show it to me, and per-haps" (he smiled and raised his eyebrows, as he slyly drawled the word "perhaps") "I'll buy it. We'll drive miles and miles away. You shall see the spring in the South. . . . Eh, Margot?"

"That's not the point," she said sulkily.

"The point is that you should be happy. And happy you'll be. Where's that hanky? We'll come back in the autumn; you shall take some more courses in film-acting, and I'll find a really clever producer for you—Grossman, for instance."

"No, not him," muttered Margot with a shudder.

"All right, another one then. And now, wipe away your tears like a good girl, and we'll go out to supper. Please, little one."

"I'll never be happy until you get a divorce," she said, sighing deeply. "But I'm afraid you'll leave me, now that you've seen me in that disgusting film. Oh, another man in your place would have slapped their faces for making me look so monstrous! No, you shan't kiss me. Tell me, have you done anything about the divorce? Or has the whole thing been dropped?"

"Well, no . . . You see, it's like this," stammered Albinus. "You . . . We . . . Oh, Margot, we have just . . . That is to say, she in particular . . . in a word, this bereavement makes it rather difficult for me."

"What's that you say?" asked Margot, rising to her feet. "Does she still not know that you want her to divorce you?"

"No, I didn't mean that," said Albinus lamely.

"Of course, she feels . . . That is to say, she knows . . . Or, better say . . ."

Margot slowly drew herself up higher and higher, like a snake when it uncoils.

"To tell the truth, she won't divorce me," said Albinus at last, for the first time in his life telling a lie about Elisabeth.

"Oh, is that so?" asked Margot, as she advanced on him.

"She's going to strike me," thought Albinus wearily.

Margot came right up to him and slowly placed her arms round his neck.

"I can't go on being only your mistress," she said, pressing her cheek against his tie, "I can't. Do something about it. Say to yourself tomorrow: I'll do it for my baby! There are lawyers. It can all be arranged."

"I promise you I'll do it this autumn," he said.

She sighed softly, walked to the mirror and languidly gazed at her own reflection.

"Divorce?" thought Albinus. "No, no, that's out of the question."

◦§ 25 §◦

Rex had converted the room which he had
rented for his meetings with Margot into a
studio, and whenever Margot came she found
him at work. He generally whistled tunefully
while he drew.

Margot gazed at his chalk-white cheeks, his
thick, crimson lips pursed into a circle as he
whistled, and she felt that this man meant everything to her. He wore a silk shirt with an open
collar and a pair of old flannel trousers. He was
performing miracles with Indian ink.

They met like this almost every afternoon,
and Margot kept putting off the day of departure,
although the car was bought and it was already
spring.

"May I offer a suggestion?" said Rex to Albinus one day. "Why do you need to take a
chauffeur for your trip? I'm rather good at driving cars, you know."

"That's very kind of you," answered Albinus,

196

rather hesitatingly. "But . . . well, I'm afraid to take you away from your work. We want to go rather a long way."

"Oh, don't bother about me. I meant to take a holiday in any case. Glorious sun . . . quaint old customs . . . golf-links . . . trips included . . ."

"In that case we shall be delighted," said Albinus, wondering anxiously what Margot would think of it. But Margot, after a little hesitation, agreed to the suggestion.

"All right, let him come," she said. "I really quite like him, but he's got into the habit of confiding his love-affairs to me, and he sighs over them as if they were the normal thing. It gets a little tedious."

It was the day before their departure. On her way home from the shops, Margot ran in to see Rex. The box of paints, the pencils, a dusty ray of sunlight slanting across the room—all this reminded her of the time when she posed in the nude.

"Why are you in such a hurry?" said Rex lazily, as she was making up her lips. "Today is the last time. I don't know how we're going to manage on the journey."

"We are both smart enough," she answered with a throaty laugh.

She ran into the street and looked for a taxi.

But the sunlit thoroughfare was empty. She came to a square—and as she always did when she was returning home from Rex's room, she thought: "Shall I turn to the right, then across the garden, and then to the right again?"

There lay the street where she had lived as a child.

(The past was safe in its cage. Why not have a look?)

The street had not changed. There was the baker's at the corner, and there was the butcher's with the gilt ox-head on the signboard, and outside the shop a bulldog was tied up—it belonged to the major's widow from No. 15. But the stationery shop had turned into a hairdresser's. There was the same old newspaper woman at her stand. There was the beer-house which Otto used to patronize; and over there was the house in which she had been born: it was undergoing repairs, judging by the scaffolding. She did not care to go any nearer.

As she was walking back, a familiar voice called to her.

It was Kaspar, her brother's companion. He was pushing a bicycle with a violet frame and a basket in front of the handlebar.

"Hullo, Margot," he said, smiling a little shyly, and he walked along the pavement by her side.

198

The last time she had seen him he had been very surly; but that had been a group, an organization, almost a gang. Now that he was alone, he was simply an old friend.

"Well, how are you getting on, Margot?"

"Splendidly," she laughed. "And what about you?"

"Oh, just rubbing along. Did you know that your people have moved? They're living in North Berlin now. You should pay them a visit one day, Margot. Your father won't hold out much longer."

"And where's my dear brother?" she asked.

"Oh, he's gone away. I fancy he's working at Bielefeld."

"You know yourself how much they loved me at home," she said, frowning at her feet, as she walked on the very edge of the curb. "And did they bother about me afterward? Did they care what became of me?"

Kaspar coughed and said:

"All the same, they're your people, Margot. Your mother got the sack here and she doesn't like the new place."

"And what do people say about me here?" she asked, looking up at him.

"Oh, a lot of rubbish. Back-biting. The usual thing. I've always said that a girl has the right to do as she likes with her own life. And are you getting on well with your friend?"

"Oh, yes, more or less. He's going to marry me soon."

"Fine," said Kaspar. "I'm very glad for your sake. Only it's a pity that it's impossible to have any fun with you, like in the old days. A great pity."

"Haven't you got a sweetheart?" she asked, smiling.

"No, not at the moment. Life's very hard sometimes, Margot. I'm working in a confectioner's. I should like to have a confectioner's shop of my own some day."

"Yes, life can be hard," said Margot pensively, and after a little pause she called a taxi.

"Perhaps one day we might—" Kaspar began; but no—they would never again bathe in that lake.

"She's going to the dogs," he thought as he watched her seat herself in the cab. "Ought to marry some good, simple man. I wouldn't take her, though. A fellow would never know where he was . . ."

He swung himself onto the bicycle and rode rapidly after the taxi to the next street corner. Margot waved to him as he swerved gracefully into a side street.

◄§ 26 §►

ROADS bordered with apple trees, and then roads with plum trees, were lapped up by the front tires—endlessly. The weather was fine, and toward night the steel cells of the radiator were crammed with dead bees, and dragon-flies, and meadow-browns. Rex drove wonderfully, reclining lazily on the very low seat and manipulating the steering wheel with a tender and almost dreamy touch. In the back-window hung a plush monkey, gazing toward the North from which they were speeding away.

Then, in France, there were poplars along the roads; the maids in the hotels did not understand Margot, and this made her wild. It was proposed that they should spend the spring on the Riviera, and then push on to the Italian lakes. Shortly before reaching the coast, their last stopping place was at Rouginard.

They arrived there at sunset. An orange-flushed cloud curled in wisps across the pale green sky, above the dark mountains; lights glowed in the squatting cafés; the plane trees on the boulevard were already shrouded in darkness.

Margot was tired and irritable, as she always was toward night. Since their departure—that is to say, for almost three weeks (for they had not hurried, stopping in a number of picturesque little places with the same old church in the same old square), she had not once been alone with Rex. When they drove into Rouginard, and Albinus was going into ecstasies over the outlines of the purpling hills, Margot muttered through her clenched teeth: "Oh, gush away, gush away." She was on the brink of tears. They drove up to a big hotel, and Albinus went to ask about rooms.

"I shall go mad if this goes on much longer," said Margot, without looking at Rex.

"Give him a sleeping draught," suggested Rex. "I'll get one from the chemist."

"I've tried already," answered Margot, "but it doesn't act."

Albinus returned a little upset.

"No good," he said. "It's very tiresome. I'm sorry, darling."

They drove to three hotels in succession, and they were all full up. Margot flatly refused to go on to the next town, as she said that the curves of the road made her sick. She was in such a temper that Albinus was afraid to look at her. At last, in the fifth hotel, they were asked to enter the lift in order to go up and see the only two rooms available. An olive-skinned lift-boy who took them up stood with his handsome profile toward them.

"Look at those eyelashes," said Rex, nudging Albinus gently.

"Stop that damfoolery," exclaimed Margot suddenly.

The room with the double bed was not at all bad, but Margot kept tapping her heel gently on the floor and repeating in a low sulky voice: "I won't stay here, I won't stay here."

"But really, it's quite nice for one night," said Albinus entreatingly.

The servant opened an inside door to the bathroom; went through and opened a second door, disclosing a second bedroom.

Rex and Margot suddenly exchanged glances.

"I don't know if you'll mind sharing the bathroom with us, Rex?" said Albinus. "Margot is rather splashy and long about it."

"Good," laughed Rex. "We'll manage somehow."

"Are you quite sure you haven't got another

single room?" asked Albinus, turning to the servant, but here Margot hurriedly intervened:

"Nonsense," she said. "It's all right. I refuse to traipse around any longer."

She walked to the window while the baggage was being brought in. There was a big star in the plum-colored sky, the black tree-tops were perfectly still, crickets chirped . . . but she saw and heard nothing.

Albinus began to unpack the toilet-things.

"I'm going to have a bath first," she said, undressing hurriedly.

"Go ahead," he answered cheerily. "I'll be shaving. But don't be too long—we must get some dinner."

In the mirror he saw Margot's jumper, skirt, a couple of light undergarments, one stocking and then the other, fly swiftly through the air.

"Little slattern," he said thickly, as he lathered his chin.

He heard the door shut, the bolts rattle and the water pour in noisily.

"You needn't lock yourself in, I'm not going to turn you out," he called out laughingly, as he stretched his cheek with his finger.

There was a loud and steady rush of water behind the locked door. Albinus carefully scraped his cheek with a heavily plated Gillette. He wondered whether they had lobsters à l'Américaine here.

The water went on rushing—and grew louder and louder. He had turned the corner, so to speak, and was about to return to his Adam's apple, where a few little bristles were always reluctant to go, when suddenly he noticed with a shock that a stream of water was trickling from beneath the door of the bathroom. The roar of the taps had now taken on a triumphant note.

"Surely she can't be drowned," he muttered, running to the door and knocking.

"Darling, are you all right? You're flooding the room!"

No answer.

"Margot, Margot!" he shouted, rattling the handle (and quite unconscious of the queer part doors played in his and her life).

Margot slipped back into the bathroom. It was full of steam and hot water. She swiftly turned off the taps.

"I went to sleep in the bath," she called out plaintively through the door.

"You're crazy," said Albinus. "How you frightened me!"

The rivulets blackening the pale gray carpet weakened and stopped. Albinus walked back to the mirror and lathered his throat once more.

In a few minutes Margot emerged fresh and radiant, and began to smother herself with talc-powder. Albinus, in his turn, went to have a bath. The place was reeking with moisture. He knocked at Rex's door.

"I won't keep you waiting," he cried. "The bath'll be free in a moment."

"Oh, take your time, take your time!" shouted Rex happily.

At supper Margot was in splendid spirits. They sat on the terrace. A white moth fluttered round the lamp and fell down on the tablecloth.

"We'll stay here a long, long time," said Margot. "I like this place tremendously."

✌ 27 ⅏

A WEEK passed, and a second. The days were
cloudless. There were lots of flowers and for-
eigners. An hour's drive took one to a beautiful
sand beach set in dark red rocks against the dark
blue sea. Pine-clad hills surrounded their hotel,
a fine building as such buildings go, in a sickening
Moorish style that would have made Albinus'
flesh creep had he not been so happy. Margot
was happy too; so was Rex.

She was much admired: by a silk manufacturer
from Lyons; by a quiet Englishman who collected
beetles; by the youths who played tennis with
her. But no matter who stared at her or danced
with her, Albinus felt no jealousy. It quite surprised him to recall the pangs he had suffered at
Solfi: why had everything made him uneasy then
and why did he feel so sure of her at present?
He did not notice one little thing: that she no
longer had any wish to please others; she needed

only one man—Rex. And Rex was Albinus' shadow.

One day the three of them went for a long ramble in the mountains, got lost, and finally came down by a difficult stony path that took them the wrong way. Margot, who was not used to walking, blistered her foot badly, and the two men carried her by turns, well-nigh crashing down with their burden, as neither was very robust. At about two in the afternoon they reached a sun-drenched little village, and found the Rouginard bus ready to start from a cobbly square where some men were playing bowls. Margot and Rex got inside, Albinus was about to do the same, but then, observing that the driver had not yet seated himself and would be some time yet helping an old farmer to get his two large crates in, he tapped on the half-open pane at which Margot was sitting and said he would make a dash for a drink. He made the dash and entered a small bar on the corner of the square. As he was reaching for his beer, he jostled against a delicate little man in white flannels who was hurriedly paying. They looked at each other.

"You here, Udo?" exclaimed Albinus. "This is an unexpected pleasure."

"Very unexpected," said Udo Conrad. "You've

grown a little balder, old man. Are you here with your family?"

"Well, no . . . You see, I'm staying at Rouginard and—"

"Good," said Conrad. "I'm living at Rouginard too. Heavens, the bus is starting. Hurry up."

"I'm coming," said Albinus, and swilled down his beer.

Conrad trotted toward the bus and boarded it. The horn tooted. Albinus fumbled with elusive French coins.

"Oh, there's no hurry," said the bartender, a melancholy man with a black drooping moustache. "It'll first go round the village and then stop again at this corner before going on."

"Ah, well," said Albinus. "Then I'll have another drink."

Through the bright doorway he saw the long, low, yellow bus speed away through a speckled maze of plane-tree shadow which seemed to mingle with it and dissolve it.

"Funny, meeting Udo," Albinus mused. "He's grown a little blond beard, as if to compensate for my loss of hair. When did we last see each other? Six years ago. Am I thrilled to see him? Not at all. I thought he lived in San Remo. A quaint, frail, rather eerie and not very happy man. Celibacy, hay-fever, hates cats and the ticking of clocks. A fine writer. A delightful writer. Funny that he hasn't the faintest idea that my life has changed. Funny, my standing here in this hot, drowsy little place where I've never been before and shall probably never come again. I wonder what Elisabeth is doing now? Black dress, idle hands. Better not think of it."

"How long does the bus take to go round the village?" he asked in his slow, careful French.

"A couple of minutes," said the bartender sadly.

"Not quite clear what they do with those wooden balls. Wooden? Or is it some metal? First cupped in the palm, then launched forward . . . rolling, stopping. Awkward if he happens to get into conversation with the little girl on the way and she blurts it all out before I tell him. Will she? I wonder. Not much chance of their talking though. She was unhappy, poor child, and will sit quite still."

"It seems to be quite a big village, judging by the time it takes to go round," he remarked.

"It doesn't go round," said an old man with a clay pipe who was sitting at a table behind him.

"It does," said the gloomy bartender.

"It did up to last Sunday," said the old man. "Now it goes straight on."

"Well," said the bartender, "that's no fault of mine, is it?"

"But what shall I do now?" cried Albinus in dismay.

"Take the next one," said the old man judiciously.

He got home at last and found Margot in a deck chair on the terrace, eating cherries, with Rex sitting on the white parapet in bathing shorts, his long hairy brown back turned to the sun. A quiet happy picture.

"I missed the blessed thing," said Albinus, grinning.

"You would," said Margot.

"Tell me, did you notice a small man in white with a goldenish beard?"

"I did," said Rex. "Sat behind us. What about him?"

"Nothing—just a man I used to know once."

⋙ 28 ⋘

THE next morning, Albinus made conscientious inquiries at the Tourist Office and then at a German boarding house, but no one could tell him Udo Conrad's address. "After all, we've nothing much to say to each other," he thought. "Probably I'll run into him again, if we stay here any longer. And if I don't, it doesn't much matter."

A few days later he woke up earlier than usual, threw open the shutters, smiled at the tender blue sky and at the soft green slopes, luminous yet hazy, as if it were all a bright frontispiece under tissue paper, and he felt a strong longing to climb and wander, and to breathe the thyme-scented air.

Margot awoke. "It's still so early," she said drowsily.

He suggested they should dress quickly and go out for the whole day—just the two of them . . .

"Go by yourself," she murmured, turning over to the other side.

"Oh, you lazybones," said Albinus sadly.

It was about eight. At a good pace, he got out of the narrow streets, cut longitudinally in two by the morning shade and sunshine, and began the ascent.

As he was passing a tiny villa, painted a warm pink, he heard the click of shears, and saw Udo Conrad pruning something in the small, rocky garden. Yes, he had always had a green thumb.

"Got you at last," said Albinus gaily, and the other turned but did not smile back.

"Oh," he said drily, "I didn't expect to see you again."

Solitude had developed in him a spinsterish touchiness, and now he was deriving a morbid pleasure from feeling hurt.

"Don't be silly, Udo," said Albinus, as he approached, gently pushing aside the feathery foliage of a mimosa tree, which leaned wistfully in his way. "You know quite well I didn't miss it on purpose. I thought it would go round the village and come back again."

Conrad softened a little. "Never mind," he said, "it often happens like that: one meets a man after a long interval and suddenly feels a panicky desire to give him the slip. I took it that you didn't

213

enjoy the prospect of having to chatter about old times in the moving prison of a bus; and you avoided it neatly."

Albinus laughed: "The truth is, I've been hunting for you these last days. Nobody seemed to know your exact whereabouts."

"Yes, I only rented this cottage a few days ago. And where are you staying?"

"Oh, at the Britannia. Really, I'm terribly glad to see you, Udo. You must tell me all about yourself."

"Shall we go for a little walk?" suggested Conrad dubiously. "All right. I'll put on some other shoes."

He was back in a minute and they started to climb up a cool shady road winding between vine-clad stone walls, its blue asphalt still untouched by the hot morning sun.

"And how's your family?" asked Conrad.

Albinus hesitated and then said:

"Better not ask, Udo. Some terrible things have been happening to me lately. Last year we separated, Elisabeth and I. And then my little Irma died from pneumonia. I prefer not to talk of these matters if you don't mind."

"How very distressing," said Conrad.

They both fell silent; Albinus pondered whether it might not be rather glamorous and exciting to talk about his passionate love-affair to

214

this old pal of his, who had always known him as a shy, unadventurous fellow; but he put it off till later. Conrad, on the other hand, was reflecting that he had made a mistake in going for this walk: he preferred people to be carefree and happy when they shared his company.

"I didn't know you were in France," said Albinus. "I thought you usually dwelt in Mussolini's country."

"Who is Mussolini?" asked Conrad with a puzzled frown.

"Ah—you're always the same," laughed Albinus. "Don't get into a panic, I'm not going to talk politics. Tell me about your work, please. Your last novel was superb."

"I'm afraid," said Udo, "that our fatherland is not quite at the right level to appreciate my writings. I'd gladly write in French, but I'm loath to part with the experience and riches amassed in the course of my handling of our language."

"Come, come," said Albinus. "There are lots of people who love your books."

"Not as I love them," said Conrad. "It'll be a long time—a solid century, perhaps—till I am appreciated at my worth. That is, if the art of writing and reading is not quite forgotten by then; and I am afraid it is being rather thoroughly forgotten this last half century, in Germany."

"How's that?" asked Albinus.

215

"Well, when a literature subsists almost exclusively on Life and Lives, it means it is dying. And I don't think much of Freudian novels or novels about the quiet countryside. You may argue that it is not literature in the mass that matters, but the two or three real writers who stand aloof, unnoticed by their grave, pompous contemporaries. All the same it is rather trying sometimes. It makes me wild to see the books that are being taken seriously."

"No," said Albinus, "I'm not at all of your mind. If our age is interested in social problems, there's no reason why authors of talent should not try to help. The War, post-War unrest—"

"Don't," moaned Conrad gently.

They were silent again. The winding road had taken them to a pine grove where the creaking of the cicadas was like the endless winding-up and whir of some clockwork toy. A stream was running over flat stones which seemed to quiver under the knots of water. They sat down on the dry, sweet-smelling turf.

"But don't you feel rather an outcast, always living abroad?" asked Albinus, as he gazed up at the pine-tops that looked like seaweeds swimming in blue water. "Don't you long for the sound of German voices?"

"Oh, well, I do run into compatriots now and

then; and it is sometimes quite amusing. I've noticed, for instance, that German tourists are inclined to think that not a soul can understand their language."

"I could not always live abroad," said Albinus, lying on his back and dreamily following with his eye the outlines of blue gulfs and lagoons and creeks between the green branches.

"That day we met," said Conrad, also reclining, with his arms under his head, "I had a rather fascinating experience with those two friends of yours in the bus. You do know them, don't you?"

"Yes, slightly," replied Albinus with a little laugh.

"So I thought, judging from their merriment at your being left behind."

("Wicked little girl," thought Albinus tenderly. "Shall I tell him all about her? No.")

"I had quite a good time listening to their conversation. But I did not feel exactly homesick. It is a queer thing: the more I think of it, the more I feel certain that there comes a time in an artist's life when he stops needing his fatherland. Like those creatures, you know, who first live in an aquatic state and then on dry land."

"There would be something in me yearning for the coolness of water," said Albinus with a sort of heavyish whimsicality. "By the way, I found a rather nice bit in the very beginning of Baum's new book *Discovery of Taprobana*. A Chinese traveler, it appears, ages ago, journeyed across Gobi to India, and stood one day by a great jade image of Buddha in a shrine on a hill in Ceylon, and saw a merchant offering a native Chinese present—a white silk fan—and—"

". . . and," interrupted Conrad, " 'a sudden weariness of his long exile seized upon the traveler.' I know that sort of thing—though I haven't read that dreary fool's last effort and never will. Anyway, the merchants I see here aren't particularly good at provoking nostalgia."

They were both silent again. Both felt very bored. After contemplating for a few minutes more the pines and the sky, Conrad sat up and said:

"You know, old boy, I'm awfully sorry, but would you mind very much if we went back? I've got some writing to get done before midday."

"Right you are," said Albinus, rising in his turn. "I must be getting home too."

They descended the path in silence and then shook hands at Conrad's door with a great show of cordiality.

"Well, that's over," thought Albinus, much relieved. "Catch me calling on him again!"

218

❧ 29 ❧

On his way home, as he was entering a *bar-tabacs* to get some cigarettes and pushing aside with the back of his hand the streaming, tinkling bead-and-reed curtain, he collided with the retired French colonel who, for the last two or three days, had been their dining room neighbor. Albinus stepped back onto the narrow sidewalk.

"Pardon," said the colonel (a hearty fellow). "Fine morning, what?"

"Very fine," agreed Albinus.

"And where are the lovers today?" inquired the colonel.

"What d'you mean?" asked Albinus.

"Well, people who cuddle in corners (*qui se pelotent dans tous les coins*) are usually called so, aren't they?" said the colonel, with what the French call a *goguenard* look in his porcelain-blue, bloodshot eye. "I only wish," he added,

219

"they wouldn't do it in the garden immediately under my window. It makes an old man envious."

"What d'you mean?" repeated Albinus.

"I don't feel equal to saying it all over again in German," laughed the colonel. "Good morning, my dear sir."

He walked away. Albinus entered the shop.

"What nonsense!" he exclaimed, staring hard at the woman who sat on a stool behind the counter.

"*Comment, Monsieur?*" she asked.

"What perfect nonsense," he repeated, as he stopped at the corner, and stood there, with knitted brows, in the way of passers-by. He had the obscure sensation of everything's being suddenly turned the other way round, so that he had to read it all backward if he wanted to understand. It was a sensation devoid of any pain or astonishment. It was simply something dark and looming, and yet smooth and soundless, coming toward him; and there he stood, in a kind of dreamy, helpless stupor, not even trying to avoid that ghostly impact, as if it were some curious phenomenon which could do him no harm so long as this stupor lasted.

"Impossible," he said suddenly—and a queer, twisted thought occurred to him; he followed its weird, bat-like shudder and flight as if, again, it were a thing to study, not to be frightened of. Then he turned round, almost knocking down a little girl in a black pinafore, and hastily went back the way he had just come.

Conrad, who had been writing in the garden, went to his study on the ground floor for a note-book he needed, and was in the act of looking for it on his desk by the window when he saw Albinus' face peering at him from outside. ("Bother the man," he thought swiftly. "Isn't he going to give me any peace now?—popping out from nowhere.")

"Look here, Udo," said Albinus in a strange, blurred kind of voice, "I forgot to ask you something. What did they talk about in the bus?"

"Pardon?" said Conrad.

"What did those two talk about in the bus? You said it was a fascinating experience."

"A what?" asked Conrad. "Oh, yes, now I see. Well, it was fascinating in a way. Yes, quite right. I wanted to give you that example of how Germans behave when they think no one can understand? Is that what you mean?"

Albinus nodded.

"Well," said Conrad, "it was the cheapest, loudest, nastiest amorous prattle that I've ever heard in my life. Those friends of yours talked as freely of their love as though they were alone in Paradise—a rather gross Paradise, I'm afraid."

"Udo," said Albinus, "can you swear to what you're saying?"

"Pardon?"

"Are you perfectly, perfectly sure of what you're saying?"

"Why, yes. What's the idea? Wait a bit, I'm coming into the garden. I can't hear a word through this window."

He found his notebook and went out. "Hullo, where are you?" he cried. But Albinus had disappeared. Conrad walked out into the lane. No—the man was gone.

"I wonder," muttered Conrad, "I wonder whether I haven't committed some blunder (. . . nasty rhyme, that! 'Was it, I wonder, a—*la*, la, la—*blunder?*' Horrible!) ."

✺ 30 ✺

ALBINUS descended into the town, crossed the boulevard without quickening his steady pace, and reached his hotel. He went up and into his room—their room. It was empty, the bed was not made; some coffee had been spilled and a little spoon was gleaming on the white rug. With bent head he gazed at that shiny spot. At that moment Margot's shrill laugh sounded from the garden below.

He leaned out of the window. She was walking by the side of a youth in white shorts, and the racket which she brandished as she chattered, glistened like gold in the sun. Her partner caught sight of Albinus at the third-floor window. Margot looked up and stopped.

Albinus moved his arm as if grabbing something to his breast: it was supposed to mean "come up" and so Margot understood it. She nodded and lazily came down the gravel walk toward the oleander shrubs which flanked the entrance.

He walked back from the window, squatted down and unlocked his suitcase, but then remembered that what he was looking for was in another place. He walked over to the wardrobe and thrust his hand into the pocket of his yellow camel's-hair overcoat. He rapidly examined the thing he had got out to see if it was loaded: then he posted himself at the door.

As soon as she opened it he would shoot her down. He would not bother to ask her any questions. It was all as plain as death and, with a kind of hideous smoothness, fitted into the logical scheme of things. They had been deceiving him steadily, astutely, artistically. She must be killed at once.

As he waited for her at the door, his mind went out to track her. Now she would have entered the hotel; now she would be coming up in the lift. He listened for the click of her heels along the corridor. But his imagination had outstripped her. Everything was silent. He must begin afresh. He held the automatic pistol and it seemed like a natural extension of his hand which was tense and eager to discharge itself: there was almost a sensual pleasure in the thought of pressing back that incurved trigger.

He almost fired at the white closed door when

224

he heard the light patter of her rubber soles—yes, of course: she was wearing tennis shoes, there were no heels to click. Now! But at that moment he heard other steps.

"Will Madame permit me to fetch the tray?" asked a French voice outside the door. Margot came in at the same time as the chambermaid. Unconsciously he slipped the pistol into his pocket.

"What d'you want?" demanded Margot. "You might have come down, you know, instead of calling me up so rudely."

He made no reply, but watched with bowed head while the chambermaid placed the crockery on the tray and picked up the little spoon. She lifted the tray, beamed, went out, and now the door closed.

"Albert, whatever has happened?"

He lowered his hand into his pocket. Margot, with a shiver of pain, dropped down on a chair by the bed, bent her sunburned neck and began to untie quickly the laces of her white shoe. He looked at her glossy black head, at the bluish shade on her neck where the hair had been shaved. Impossible to fire while she was taking off her shoe. She had a sore place just above her heel and the blood had soaked through her white sock.

"It's absurd how badly I rub it every time,"

she said, lifting her head. She saw the black gun in his hand.

"Don't play with that thing, you fool," she said very calmly.

"Stand up," whispered Albinus, and clutched her wrist.

"I won't stand up," answered Margot, pulling the sock off with her free hand. "Let me go. Look, it's got stuck to the sock."

He shook her so violently that the chair rattled. She gripped the edge of the bedstead and began to laugh.

"Please, shoot me, do," she said. "It will be just like that play we saw, with the nigger and the pillow, and I'm just as innocent as she was."

"You lie," whispered Albinus. "You and that scoundrel. Nothing but trickery and de-de-deceit, and . . ." His upper lip trembled. He struggled with his stammer.

"Please, put that thing down. I won't speak to you until you have. I don't know what's happened and I don't want to. I only know one thing: I am faithful to you, I am faithful . . ."

"All right," said Albinus hoarsely. "You can say what you have to say. But after that you shall die."

"You need not kill me—really, you needn't, darling."

226

"Go on. Speak."

(". . . if I were to rush to the door," she thought, "I might just manage to run out. Then I'd scream, and people would come running up. But then everything would be spoiled—everything . . .")

"I can't speak as long as you're holding that thing. Please, put it away."

(". . . or perhaps I could knock it out of his hand? . . .")

"No," said Albinus. "First of all, you must confess . . . I've got information. I know all . . . I know all . . ." he repeated in a broken voice, walking up and down the room and striking the furniture with the edge of his palm. "I know all. He sat behind you in that bus, and you behaved like lovers. Oh, of course, I shall shoot you."

"Yes, I thought as much," said Margot. "I knew that you wouldn't understand. For God's sake, put that thing down, Albert."

"What is there to understand?" screamed Albinus. "What is there to be explained?"

"In the first place, Albert, you know very well that he doesn't care for women."

"Shut up!" screamed Albinus. "That was a base lie, a rascally trick from the beginning."

("If he yells—the danger is over," thought Margot.)

"No. He really doesn't care for women," she went on, "but once—for a joke—I suggested to him: 'Look here, let's see whether I can't make you forget your boys.' Oh, we both knew it was only a joke. That was all, that was all, darling."

"A dirty lie. I don't believe it. Conrad saw you. That French colonel saw you. Only I was blind."

"Oh, but I often teased him that way," said Margot coolly. "It was all very funny. But I won't any more, if it upsets you."

"So you deceived me only for a joke? How filthy!"

"Of course, I didn't deceive you! How dare you say such a thing. He wouldn't have been capable of helping me to deceive you. We didn't even kiss: even that would have been repulsive to both of us."

"And if I questioned him—not in your presence, of course, not in your presence?"

"Do, by all means. He'll tell you exactly the same. Only you'll make yourself rather ridiculous."

They went on talking in this way for an hour. Margot was gradually getting the upper hand. But at length she could stand it no longer and had a fit of hysterics. She threw herself onto the bed in her white tennis frock, with one foot bare, and, as she gradually calmed down, she wept into the pillows.

228

Albinus sat in a chair by the window; outside the sun was shining and gay English voices floated across from the tennis-ground. Mentally he reviewed every least episode from the beginning of their acquaintanceship with Rex, and among them some were touched by that livid light which had now spread over his whole existence. Something was destroyed forever; no matter how convincingly Margot tried to prove that she had been faithful to him, everything would henceforward be tainted with a poisonous flavor of doubt.

At length he rose to his feet, walked across to the bed, gazed at her pink wrinkled heel with the bit of black plaster on it—when had she managed to stick it on?—gazed at the golden brown skin of her slim but firm calf, and reflected that he could kill her, but that he could not part from her.

"Very well, Margot," he said gloomily. "I believe you. But you must get up immediately and change your clothes. We're going to pack our things at once and leave this place. I'm not physically equal to meeting him now—I can't answer for myself. Not because I believe that you have deceived me with him, no, not on that account, but I simply can't do it; I've pictured it all to myself too vividly, and . . . well, no matter . . . Come, get up . . ."

"Kiss me," said Margot softly.

"No; not now. I want to get away from here as soon as possible . . . I almost shot you in this room, and I shall certainly shoot you if we don't pack our things at once—at once."

"As you like," said Margot. "But please remember that you've insulted me and my love for you in the worst manner possible. I suppose you'll understand that later."

Swiftly and silently, without looking at each other, they packed. Then the porter came for the luggage.

Rex was playing poker with a couple of Americans and a Russian on the terrace, in the shade of a giant eucalyptus. Luck was against him that morning. He was just contemplating doing a little palming at his next shuffle, or perhaps using in a certain private manner the mirror inside his cigarette-case lid (little tricks that he disliked and used only when playing with tyros), when suddenly beyond the magnolias, in the road near the garage, he saw Albinus' car. The car swerved awkwardly and disappeared.

"What's up?" murmured Rex. "Who's driving that car?"

He paid his debts and went to look for Margot. She was not on the tennis-ground, she was not in the garden. He went upstairs. Albinus' door was ajar. The room was dead, the open wardrobe empty; empty, too, the glass shelf above the washstand. A torn and crumpled newspaper lay on the floor.

Rex pulled at his underlip and passed into his own room. He thought—rather vaguely—that he might find a note there with some explanation. There was nothing, of course. He clicked his tongue and went down into the hall—to find out whether, at least, they had paid for his room.

⋅§ 31 ⧽⋅

THERE are a great many people who, without possessing any expert knowledge, are yet able to readjust an electrical connection after the mysterious occurrence known as a "short circuit"; or, with the aid of a penknife, to set a watch going again; or even, if necessary, to fry a cutlet. Albinus was not one of them. He could not tie a dress-tie nor pare his right-hand nails, nor make up a parcel; he could not uncork a bottle without picking to bits one half of the cork, and drowning the other. As a child he never built things like other boys. As a youth he had never taken his bicycle to pieces, nor, indeed, could do anything with it save ride it; and when he punctured a tire, he pushed the disabled machine—squelching like an old galosh—to the nearest repair shop. Later, when he studied the restoration of pictures, he was always afraid to touch the canvas himself.

During the War he had distinguished himself by an amazing incapacity to do anything whatever with his hands. In view of all this it is less surprising that he was a very bad driver than that he could drive at all.

Slowly and with difficulty (and a complicated argument, the gist of which he failed to catch, with the policeman at the crossroads) he got his car out of Rouginard and then accelerated a little.

"Do you mind telling me where we are going, if you don't mind?" asked Margot tartly.

He shrugged his shoulders and stared straight ahead along the shiny blue-black road. Now that they were out of Rouginard, where the narrow streets had been full of people and traffic and where he had had to sound his horn, pull up with a jerk and turn clumsily—now that they were bowling smoothly along the highway, various thoughts drifted darkly and confusedly through his brain; that the road climbed up and up into the mountains and that it would soon begin to wind dangerously, that Rex's button had once got entangled in Margot's lace and that his heart had never been so heavy and distraught as now.

"It's all one to me where we go," said Margot, "but I'd just like to know. And please do keep to the right. If you can't drive, we had better take a train or hire a chauffeur at the nearest garage."

He put on the brake violently because a motor coach had appeared in the distance.

"What are you doing, Albert? Keep to the right, that's all you've got to do."

The motor coach, filled with tourists, thundered past. Albinus started off again. The road began to curve round the mountain.

"Does it matter where we go?" He thought, "Wherever we go, I shall not escape this pain. 'The cheapest, loudest, nastiest—' I shall go mad."

"I won't ask you again," said Margot, "but for God's sake don't wobble before the bends. It is ridiculous. What are you trying to do? If you knew how my head aches. I shall be thankful when we get *somewhere*."

"You swear to me there was nothing in it?" asked Albinus in a faint voice, and he felt hot tears dimming his vision. He blinked, and the road reappeared.

"I swear," said Margot. "I'm tired of swearing to you. Kill me, but don't torture me any longer. By the way, I'm too hot. I think I'll take off my coat."

He put on the brake.

Margot laughed. "What need is there to stop for that? Oh, dear, oh, dear."

He helped her out of her dustcoat and, as he

did so, he recalled with extraordinary vividness how—long, long ago—he had noticed for the first time, in a wretched little café, the way she moved her shoulders and bent her lovely neck while she wriggled out of the sleeves.

Now the tears streamed down his cheeks uncontrollably. Margot put her arms round him and pressed her temple to his bent head.

Their car was standing close to the parapet, a stout stone wall a foot high, behind which a ravine, overgrown with brambles, sloped steeply down. Far below could be heard the swish and rumble of a rapid stream. On the left-hand side rose a reddish rocky slope with pine trees on its summit. The sun was scorching. A little way ahead a man with black spectacles was sitting on the edge of the road breaking stones.

"I love you so much," groaned Albinus, "so much."

He fondled her hands and stroked her convulsively. She laughed softly—a satisfied laugh.

"Let me drive now," begged Margot. "You know I can do it better than you."

"No, I'm improving," he said, smiling, gulping, blowing his nose. "It's curious, but I really don't know where we are going. I think I've sent the luggage on to San Remo, but I'm not quite sure."

He started the engine and they drove on. It

seemed to him that the car now traveled more easily and obediently and he no longer clutched the steering wheel so nervously. The bends became more and more frequent. On one side soared the steep cliff; on the other was the ravine. The sun stabbed his eyes. The pointer of the speedometer trembled and rose.

A sharp bend was approaching and Albinus proposed to take it with special dexterity. High above the road an old woman who was gathering herbs saw to the right of the cliff this little blue car speed toward the bend, behind the corner of which, dashing from the opposite side, toward an unknown meeting, two cyclists crouched over their handlebars.

ᴀᵹ 32 ᵷᴀ

THE old woman gathering herbs on the hill-
side saw the car and the two cyclists approaching
the sharp bend from opposite directions. From
a mail plane flying coastward through the sparkling blue dust of the sky, the pilot could see
the loops of the road, the shadow of his wings
gliding across the sunlit slopes and two villages
twelve miles distant from one another. Perhaps
by rising still higher it would be possible to see
simultaneously the mountains of Provence, and
a distant town in another country—let us say, *nice!*
Berlin—where the weather was hot too; for on
this particular day the cheek of the earth from
Gibraltar to Stockholm was painted with mellow
sunshine.

In Berlin, on this particular day, a great many
ices were sold. Irma had once used to look on
with the gravity of greed when the ice-cream man
smeared a thin wafer with the thick yellowish

237

substance which, when tasted, made one's tongue dance and one's front teeth ache deliciously. So that, when Elisabeth stepped onto the balcony and noticed one of these ice-cream vendors, it seemed strange to her that he should be dressed all in white and she all in black.

She had awakened feeling very restless, and now she realized with a strange dismay that, for the first time, she had emerged from that state of dull torpor to which she had grown accustomed of late, and she could not understand why she felt so strangely uncomfortable. She lingered on the balcony and thought of the day before, on which nothing special had happened: the usual drive to the churchyard, bees settling on her flowers, the damp glitter of the box hedge round the grave; the stillness and the soft earth.

"What can it be?" she wondered. "Why am I all a-tingle?"

From the balcony she could see the ice-cream vendor with his white cap. The balcony seemed to soar higher, higher. The sun threw a dazzling light on the tiles—in Berlin, in Brussels, in Paris and farther toward the South. The mail plane was flying to St. Cassien. The old woman was gathering herbs on the rocky slope. For a whole year at least she would be telling people how she had seen . . . what she had seen. . . .

238

⤳ 33 ⤆

ALBINUS was not clear when and how he came
to know these things: the time from his blithely
taking that bend until now (a couple of weeks),
the place where he was (a clinic at Grasse), the
operation which he had undergone (trepanning),
and the reason of his long period of unconscious-
ness (effusion of blood into the brain). A moment had arrived, however, when all these bits
of information had been gathered into one—he
was alive, was fully conscious and knew that Margot and a hospital nurse were close at hand. He
felt that he had been dozing pleasantly and that
he had just awakened. But what the time was, he
did not know. Probably it was still early in the
morning.

His forehead and his eyes were covered with
a soft, thick bandage. But his skull was already
uncovered and it was strange to feel with his fingers the bristles of the new hair on his head. In

his memory he retained a picture that was, in its gaudy intensity, like a colored photograph on glass: the curve of the glossy blue road, the green and red cliff to the left, the white parapet to the right and in front of him the approaching cyclists —two dusty apes in orange-colored jerseys. A sharp jerk of the steering wheel to avoid them— and up the car dashed, mounting a pile of stones on the right, and in the next fraction of that second, a telegraph post loomed in front of the windscreen. Margot's outstretched arm had flown across the picture—and the next moment the magic lantern went out.

This recollection had been completed by Margot. Yesterday, or the day before yesterday, or even earlier—she had told him, or rather her voice—why only her voice? Why was it so long since he had really seen her? This bandage. Probably they would soon take it off . . . What had Margot's voice told him?

". . . If it had not been for the telegraph post, we should have plunged over the parapet and into the precipice. It was appalling. I've still a huge bruise on my hip. The car turned a somersault and smashed like an egg. It cost . . . le car . . . mille . . . beaucoup mille marks" (this was meant, apparently, for the nurse). "Albert, what's the French for twenty thousand?"

"Oh, what does it matter . . . You are alive!"

"The cyclists were very nice. They helped to gather up all the things. But they couldn't find the tennis rackets."

Tennis rackets? Sun on a tennis racket. Why was that so unpleasant? Oh, yes, that nightmare business at Rouginard. He with his gun in his hand. She coming in on rubber soles . . . Nonsense—all that had been cleared up, everything was all right. . . . What time was it? When would the bandage be taken off? When could he get up? Had it got into the papers—the German papers?

He turned his head this way and that; the bandage worried him. Also—the discrepancy between his senses. His ears had been absorbing so many impressions all this time, and his eyes none at all. He did not know what the room, or the nurse, or the doctor looked like. And the time? Was it morning? He had had a long, sweet sleep. Probably the window was open, for he heard the clatter of horse hoofs outside; there was also the sound of running water and the clanging note of a pail. Perhaps there was a courtyard with a well and the cool morning shade of plane trees.

He lay for some time motionless, endeavoring to transform the incoherent sound into corresponding shapes and colors. It was the opposite of trying to imagine the kind of voices which Botticelli's angels had. Presently he heard Margot's laugh and then that of the hospital nurse. Apparently they were sitting in the next room. She was teaching Margot to pronounce correctly in French: "*Soucoupe, soucoupe*"—Margot repeated several times and they both laughed softly.

Feeling that he was doing something absolutely forbidden, Albinus cautiously drew up the bandage and peeped out. But the room still remained quite dark. He could not even see the bluish glimmer of a window or those faint patches of light which come to stay with the walls at night. So it was night after all, not morning, not even early morning. A black moonless night. How deceptive sounds could be. Or were the blinds especially thick?

From the next room came a pleasant rattle of crockery: "*Café aimé toujours, thé nicht toujours.*"

Albinus fumbled over the bedside table until he felt the little electric lamp. He pressed the switch once, a second time, but the darkness remained there, as if it were too heavy to move. Probably the plug had been taken out. He felt with his fingers for matches and actually found a box. There was only one match inside; he struck

242

it, heard it sizzle slightly as though it had lit, but he could not see any flame. He threw it away and suddenly smelled a faint odor of sulphur. Strange.

"Margot," he shouted suddenly, "Margot!"

A sound of rapid footsteps and of a door opening. But nothing changed. How could it be dark behind the door, if they were having coffee there?

"Turn on the light," he said angrily. "Please, turn on the light."

"You are a bad boy," said Margot's voice. He heard her approaching swiftly and surely through absolute night. "You ought not to touch that bandage."

"What do you mean? You seem to see me," he stammered. "How can you see me? Turn on the light, do you hear? At once!"

"*Calmez-vous.* Don't excite yourself," said the voice of the nurse.

These sounds, these footsteps and voices seemed to be moving on a different plane. He was here and they were somewhere else, but still, in some unaccountable way, close at hand. Between them and the night which enveloped him was an impenetrable wall. He rubbed his eyelids, turned his head this way and that, jerked himself about, but it was impossible to force a way through this solid darkness which was like a part of himself.

"It can't be!" said Albinus with the emphasis of despair. "I'm going mad! Open the window, do something!"

"The window is open," she answered softly.

"Perhaps there is no sun . . . Margot, perhaps I might see something in very sunny weather. The merest glimmer. Perhaps, with glasses."

"Lie still, my dear. The sun *is* shining, it is a glorious morning. Albert, you hurt me."

"I . . . I . . ." Albinus drew a deep breath which seemed to make his chest swell into some vast monstrous globe full of a whirling roar which presently he let out, lustily, steadily . . . And when it had all gone, he started filling up again.

◄§ 34 ᠔►

His cuts and bruises healed, his hair grew
again, but the terrible sense of this solid black
wall remained unchanged. After those paroxysms
of deadly horror, when he had howled, flung himself about and tried frantically to tear something
away from his eyes, he lapsed into a state of semi-
consciousness. Then presently there would loom
up once more that unbearable mountain of op-
pression, which was only comparable with the
panic of one who wakes to find himself in his
grave.

Gradually, however, these fits became less frequent. For hours on end he lay on his back, silent
and motionless, listening to daytime sounds,
which seemed to have turned their backs upon
him in merry converse with others. Suddenly he
would recall that morning at Rouginard—which
had really been the beginning of it all—and then
he groaned anew. He visualized the sky, blue dis-

tances, light and shade, pink houses dotting a bright green slope, lovely dream-landscapes at which he had gazed so little, so little . . .

While he was still at that hospital, Margot had read aloud to him a letter from Rex which ran as follows:

"I don't know, my dear Albinus, what staggered me most—the wrong you did me by your inexplicable and very uncivil departure, or the misfortune which has befallen you. But although you have wounded me deeply, I sympathize with you wholeheartedly in your misfortune, especially when I think of your love for painting and for those beauties of color and line which make sight the prince of all our senses.

"I am traveling today from Paris to England and thence to New York, and it will be some time before I see Germany again. Please convey my friendly greetings to your companion, whose fickle and spoiled nature was presumably the cause of your disloyalty toward me. Alas, she is only constant in relation to herself; but, like so many women, she has a craving to be admired by others, which turns to spite when the man in question, by reason of his plain-spokenness, his repulsive exterior and unnatural inclinations, cannot but excite her ridicule and aversion.

"Believe me, Albinus, I liked you well, more

than I ever showed; but if you had told me in plain terms that my presence had become irksome to you both, I should have prized your frankness highly, and then the happy recollections of our talks about painting, of our rambles in the world of color, would not have been so sadly darkened by the shadow of your faithless flight."

"Yes, that is the letter of a homosexual," said Albinus. "But all the same I'm glad he's gone. Perhaps, Margot, God has punished me for distrusting you, but woe betide you if . . ."

"If what, Albert? Go on, finish your sentence . . ."

"No. Nothing. I believe you. Oh, I believe you."

He was silent, and then he began to make that smothered sound—half moan, half bellow—which was always the beginning of his paroxysms of horror at the darkness surrounding him.

"The prince of all our senses," he repeated several times in a faltering voice. "Ah, yes, the prince . . ."

When he had calmed down, Margot said that she was going out to the travel agency. She kissed his cheek and then tripped swiftly along the shady side of the street.

She entered a cool little restaurant and seated herself next to Rex. He was drinking white wine.

"Well," he asked, "what did the poor beggar say to the letter? Didn't I word it cutely?"

"Yes, it went down all right. On Wednesday we are leaving for Zurich to see that specialist. Please, see about the tickets. But please take yours in a different carriage—it's safer."

"I'm doubtful," remarked Rex carelessly, "whether they'll let me have the tickets for nothing."

Margot smiled tenderly and began taking out notes from her handbag.

"And as a general thing," added Rex, "it would be much simpler if *I* were the cashier."

◆§ 35 §◆

ALTHOUGH Albinus had several times—in the depths of a night which employed the bright small-talk of daylight—been for a walk, a pitifully hesitating walk along the scrunching gravel paths of the hospital garden, he proved to be very ill-prepared for the journey to Zurich. At the railway station his head began to swim—and there is no stranger, more helpless sensation than that of a blind man when his head is going round. He was stunned by all the different sounds, footsteps, voices, wheels, viciously sharp and strong things which all seemed to be rushing at him, so that every second was filled with the fear of knocking against something, although Margot was guiding him.

In the train he felt his gorge rise with nausea, because he could not harmonize the clatter and rocking of the carriage with any forward motion, no matter how hard he tried to imagine the landscape which, surely, was speeding past. And then again, at Zurich, he had to make his way among invisible people and objects—obstacles and angles, which held their breath before hitting him.

"Oh, come on, don't be afraid," said Margot irritably. "I'm leading you. Now stop. We are just going to get into the taxi. Now lift your foot. Can't you be a little less timid? Really, you might be a two-year-old."

The professor, a famous oculist, made a thorough examination of Albinus' eyes. He had a soft unctuous voice so that Albinus pictured him as an old man with a clean-shaven priestlike face, although in reality, he was still fairly young and sported a bristly moustache. He repeated what Albinus for the most part already knew: that the optic nerves had been damaged at the point of their intersection in the brain. Possibly this contusion might heal; possibly complete atrophy might ensue—the chances were obscurely even. But in any case, in the patient's present condition, a thorough rest was the most important thing. A sanatorium in the mountains would be perfect. "And then we shall see," said the professor.

"Shall we see?" repeated Albinus, with a melancholy smile.

The idea of a sanatorium did not appeal to

Margot. An old Irish couple whom they met in the hotel offered to let them a small chalet just above a fashionable mountain resort. She consulted Rex and then (leaving Albinus with a hired nurse) traveled in his company to see what the place was like. It turned out to be quite nice: a small two-storied cottage with clean little rooms and a cup for holy water affixed to every door.

Rex found its position to his liking: all alone, high upon a slope amid dense black fir trees, and only a quarter of an hour's downhill walk to the village and the hotels. He chose for himself the sunniest room in the upper story. A cook was engaged in the village. Rex talked to her very impressively:

"We are offering you such high wages," he said, "because you'll be in the service of a man who is blinded as the result of a violent mental shock. I'm the doctor in charge of him, but in view of his state of mind he must *not* know that a doctor is living in the house with him as well as his niece. If, therefore, you breathe the slightest hint, direct or indirect, as to my presence—addressing me, for instance, in his hearing, you'll be responsible in the eyes of the law for all the consequences of interrupting the progress of his recovery, and such conduct is, I believe, very severely punished in Switzerland. Moreover, I advise you not to come near my patient, or indeed to engage in any sort of conversation with him. He is subject to fits of the most violent insanity. You may be interested to know that he has already seriously injured one old woman (much like you in many respects, though not so attractive) by stamping on her face. Somehow, I should not care for such a thing to happen again. And most important of all, if you gossip about things in the village with the result that people become curious, my patient might, in his present condition, smash up everything in the house, beginning with your head. Do you get me?"

The woman was so terrified that she almost refused this extraordinarily well-paid post, and made up her mind to accept it only when Rex assured her that she would not see the blind man, his niece serving him, and that he was quite peaceable if left undisturbed. He also made arrangements with her that no butcher's boy or washerwoman should ever be allowed to penetrate the grounds. This done, Margot traveled back to fetch Albinus, while Rex moved into the house. He brought with him all the luggage, decided how the rooms were to be allotted and arranged that every superfluous breakable object should be removed. Then he went to his room and whistled tunefully as he fastened some rather improper pen-and-ink drawings to the wall.

Toward five o'clock he looked through a pair of field glasses and saw, far below, a hired motor-car approaching. Margot in a brilliant red jumper skipped out and helped Albinus to alight. With hunched shoulders, in dark spectacles, he looked like an owl. The car turned round and disappeared behind a thickly wooded bend.

Margot took the meek, clumsy man by the arm, and he climbed the footpath holding his stick in front of him. They vanished behind some fir trees, reappeared, vanished again and at length emerged upon the little garden terrace where the gloomy cook (who, incidentally, was already whole-heartedly devoted to Rex) went timorously to meet them and, trying not to look at the dangerous lunatic, relieved Margot of her attaché case.

Rex, meanwhile, leaned out of the window and made droll gestures of greeting to Margot: he pressed his hand to his heart and flung out his arms jerkily—it was a capital imitation of Punch— all this of course in dumb show, though he could have squeaked remarkably in more favorable circumstances. Margot smiled up at him and entered the house, still leading Albinus by the arm.

253

"Take me through all the rooms and describe everything to me," said Albinus. He was not really interested, but he thought that it would give Margot pleasure: she loved settling in a new place.

"A little dining room; a little drawing room, a little study," she explained, as she steered him through the ground floor. Albinus touched the furniture, patted the different objects as if they were the heads of strange children, and tried to get his bearings.

"So the window is over there," he said, pointing trustfully at a blank wall. He collided painfully with the edge of a table and tried to pretend that he had done it on purpose—groping over it with his hands, as though he wanted to take its measure.

Then they climbed side by side up the creaking wooden staircase. Above, on the top step, sat Rex, convulsed with soundless mirth. Margot shook her finger at him; he stood up cautiously and stepped back on the tips of his toes. This was really superfluous, for the staircase creaked deafeningly under the blind man's tread.

They turned into the passage. Rex, who had now retreated to his door, crouched down several times and pressed his hand to his mouth. Margot shook her head angrily—a dangerous game; he was larking about like a schoolboy.

"This is my bedroom, and here's yours," she said.

"Why not one?" asked Albinus wistfully.

"Oh, Albert," she sighed. "You know what the doctor said."

When they had been everywhere (except into Rex's room, of course) Albinus tried to go through the house without her help, just to show her how splendidly she had made him see it all. But almost at once he lost his way, ran into a wall, smiled apologetically, and nearly smashed a wash-basin. He also strayed into the corner room (which Rex had appropriated and which could only be entered from the passage), but he was already so confused that he thought he was coming out of the bathroom.

"Careful, that's a lumber-room," said Margot. "You're going to break your head. Now turn around and try to walk straight to bed. And really I don't know whether all this roaming is good for you. Don't imagine that I shall let you go on exploring like this; today is just an exception."

As it was, he already felt utterly exhausted. Margot tucked him in and brought him his supper. When he had gone to sleep she joined Rex. As they were not yet on speaking terms with the acoustics of the house, they talked in whispers. But they could just as well have spoken aloud: Albinus' bedroom was far enough away.

◦§ 36 §◦

THE impenetrable black shroud in which Albinus now lived infused an element of austerity and even of nobility into his thoughts and feelings. He was separated by darkness from that former life which had been suddenly extinguished at its sharpest bend. Remembered scenes peopled the picture gallery of his mind: Margot in a figured apron drawing aside a purple curtain (how he yearned for its dingy color now!); Margot under the shining umbrella tripping through crimson puddles; Margot naked in front of the wardrobe mirror gnawing at a yellow roll; Margot in her glistening bathing suit throwing a ball; Margot in a silvery evening gown, with her sunburned shoulders.

Then he thought of his wife, and his life with her seemed now to be steeped in a pale subdued light, and only occasionally did something emerge from this milky haze: her fair hair in the lamp glow, the light on a picture frame, Irma playing with glass marbles (a rainbow in every one), and then haze again—and Elisabeth's quiet, almost floating, movements.

Everything, even what was saddest and most shameful in his past life, was overlaid with the deceptive charm of colors. He was horrified to realize how little he had used his eyes—for these colors moved across too vague a background and their outlines were singularly blurred. If, for instance, he recalled a landscape in which he had once lived, he could not name a single plant except oaks and roses, nor a single bird save sparrows and crows, and even these were more akin to heraldry than to nature. Albinus now became conscious that he had not really been different from a certain narrow specialist at whom he used to scoff: from the workman who knows only his tools, or the virtuoso who is only a fleshly accessory of his violin. Albinus' speciality had been his passion for art; his most brilliant discovery had been Margot. But now, all that was left of her was a voice, a rustle and a perfume; it was as though she had returned to the darkness of the little cinema from which he had once withdrawn her.

But Albinus could not always console himself with esthetic or moral reflections; could not always succeed in convincing himself that physical blindness was spiritual vision; in vain did he try to cheat himself with the fancy that his life with Margot was now happier, deeper and purer, and in vain did he concentrate on the thought of her touching devotion. Of course it was touching, of course she was better than the most loyal wife—this invisible Margot, this angelic coolness, this voice which begged him not to excite himself. But no sooner had he seized her hand in the darkness, no sooner did he try to express his gratitude, than there was suddenly kindled in him such a longing to see her that all his moralizing dissolved away.

Rex was very fond of sitting in a room with him and watching his movements. Margot, as she pressed herself to the blind man's breast, pushing away at his shoulder, would cast up her eyes to the ceiling with a comical expression of resignation or put out her tongue at Albinus—this was particularly amusing in contrast with the wild and tender expression of the blind man's face. Then Margot freed herself by a dexterous movement, and retreated toward Rex, who was seated on the window sill, in white trousers, with his long-toed feet and his torso bare—he loved roasting his back in the sun. Albinus reclined in an armchair, clad in his pyjamas and dressing-gown.

258

His face was covered with bristly hair; a pink scar glistened on his temple; he looked like a bearded convict.

"Margot, come to me," he said imploringly, stretching out his arms.

Now and then Rex, who loved taking risks, went up quite close to Albinus on the tips of his bare toes and touched him with the utmost delicacy. Albinus uttered an affectionate purring sound and tried to embrace the supposed Margot while Rex side-stepped noiselessly and went back to the window sill—his habitual perch.

"My darling, do come to me," groaned Albinus, floundering out of his armchair and wading toward her. Rex on the window sill drew up his legs and Margot screamed at Albinus, declaring that she would leave him at once with a nurse if he did not do as she told him. So he shuffled back to his seat with a guilty grin.

"All right, all right," he sighed. "Read something aloud to me. The paper."

She once more cast her eyes to the ceiling.

Rex seated himself cautiously on the sofa and took Margot on his knees. She spread out the newspaper and, after patting it and poring over it, began to read aloud. Albinus nodded his head now and then and slowly consumed invisible cherries, spitting the invisible stones into his fist.

Rex mimicked Margot, pursing his lips and then drawing them in again as she did when she was reading. Or he pretended he was just going to let her fall, so that suddenly her voice would jump and she had to search for the end of the snapped sentence.

"Yes, perhaps it's all for the best," thought Albinus. "Our love is now purer and loftier. If she sticks to me now, it means that she really loves me. That is good, that is good." And suddenly he began to sob aloud, he wrung his hands and begged her to take him to another specialist, to a third, to a fourth—an operation, torture—anything that might restore his sight.

Rex, with a silent yawn, took a handful of cherries from the bowl on the table and departed to the garden.

During the first days of their life together, Rex and Margot were cautious enough, although they indulged in various harmless jests. Before the door leading from his room into the corridor Rex had erected, in case of emergency, a barricade of boxes and trunks, over which Margot clambered at night. However, after his first stroll through the house, Albinus was no longer interested in the topography of it, but he had quite got his bearings in his bedroom and in the study.

Margot described all the colors to him—the

blue wallpaper, the yellow blinds—but, egged on *new*
by Rex, she changed all the colors. The fact that
the blind man was obliged to picture his little
world in the hues prescribed by Rex afforded the
latter exquisite amusement.

In his own rooms Albinus almost had the feeling that he could see the furniture and the various
objects, and this gave him a sense of security.
But when he was sitting in the garden he felt himself surrounded by a vast unknown, because everything was too big, too unsubstantial and too full
of sounds to enable him to form a picture of it.
He tried to sharpen his hearing and to divine
movements from sound. Soon it became quite
difficult for Rex to come in or go out unnoticed.
No matter how noiselessly he passed, Albinus
turned his head at once in that direction and
asked: "Is that you, darling?" and was vexed at
his miscalculation if Margot answered him from
quite another corner.

The days passed and the more keenly Albinus
strained his hearing, the more daring did Rex
and Margot become: they accustomed themselves to the safety curtain of his blindness, and,
instead of having his meals under the adoring
dumb gaze of old Emilia in the kitchen as he
had done at first, Rex now contrived to sit at
table with both of them. He ate with a masterly

noiselessness, never touching his plate with knife or fork, and munching like a silent film diner, in perfect rhythm with Albinus' moving jaws and to the bright music of Margot's voice who purposely talked very loudly while the men chewed and swallowed. Once he choked himself: Albinus, for whom Margot was just pouring out a cup of coffee, suddenly heard at the far end of the table a strange bursting sound, an ignoble sputter. Margot promptly began to chatter, but he interrupted her, his hand raised: "What was that? What was that?"

Rex had taken his plate and moved away on tiptoe holding the napkin to his mouth. But as he was slipping through the half-open door he dropped a fork.

Albinus swung round in his chair. "What's that? Who's there?" he repeated.

"Oh, it's only Emilia. Why are you so jumpy?"

"But she never comes in here."

"Well, today she did!"

"I thought that my ears were beginning to get hallucinations," said Albinus. "Yesterday, for instance, I had the most definite impression that someone was stealing barefoot along the corridor."

"You'll go out of your mind, if you're not careful," said Margot drily.

262

In the afternoon, during Albinus' usual nap, she would sometimes go for a stroll with Rex. They fetched the letters and newspapers from the post office, or climbed up to the waterfall—and a couple of times went to a café in the pretty little town lower down. Once, as they were returning to the house and already tackling the steep footpath which led to the cottage, Rex said:

"I advise you not to insist on marriage. I'm very much afraid that, just because he deserted his wife, he has come to look upon her as a precious saint painted on glass. He will not care to smash that particular church-window. It's a simpler and better plan to get hold of his fortune gradually."

"Well, we've collected quite a large bit of it, haven't we?"

"You must get him to sell that land he has in Pomerania and his pictures," continued Rex, "or else one of his houses in Berlin. With a little cunning we could manage it. For the time being the checkbook answers the purpose admirably. He signs everything like a machine—but his bank account will soon run dry. We must hurry up, too. It would be nice to leave him, say, this winter; and before we go we'll buy him a dog—as a small token of our gratitude."

263

"Don't talk so loud," said Margot, "we're at the stone already."

This stone, a large gray one, which was overgrown with convolvulus and looked like a sheep, marked the boundary beyond which it was dangerous to talk at all. So they walked on in silence and after a few minutes were near the garden gate. Margot laughed suddenly and pointed to a squirrel. Rex chucked a stone at the animal, but missed it.

"Oh, kill it—they do a lot of damage to the trees," said Margot softly.

"Who does damage to the trees?" asked a loud voice. It was Albinus.

He was standing—rocking slightly—among the syringa shrubs on a little stone step which led from the footpath onto the lawn.

"Margot, whom are you talking to down there?" he went on. Suddenly he stumbled, dropped his stick and sat down heavily on the step.

"How dare you wander so far by yourself?" she exclaimed and, seizing him roughly, she helped him to get up. Some little bits of gravel had stuck to his hand; he spread out his fingers and tried to rub the gravel off, as a child might do.

"I wanted to catch a squirrel," declared Margot, thrusting the stick into his hand. "What did you think I was doing?"

"I fancied . . ." Albinus began. "Who's there?" he cried sharply, nearly losing his balance again as he veered in the direction of Rex, who was cautiously walking across the lawn.

"There's no one here," said Margot, "I'm alone. Why are you in such a state?" She felt her patience going.

"Lead me back to the house," he said, almost in tears. "There are too many sounds here. Trees, wind, squirrels, and things I cannot name. I don't know what's happening round me . . . It's all so noisy."

"From now on you shall be shut in," she said, and dragged him into the house.

Then, as usual, the sun went down behind the neighboring ridge. As usual, Margot and Rex sat side by side on the sofa and smoked, and half a dozen feet away from them sat Albinus in his leather armchair, staring at them fixedly with his milky blue eyes. At his request Margot told him about her childhood. She rather liked doing it. He went to bed early, slowly climbing the staircase and feeling for every step with toe and stick.

In the middle of the night he woke up and fingered the unglazed dial of an alarm clock until he found out the position of the hands. It was about half past one. He was filled with a strange uneasiness. Of late something had hindered him from concentrating on those grave and beautiful thoughts which alone were capable of shielding him against the horrors of blindness.

He lay and thought: "What is it? Elisabeth? No, she is far away. She is very far below, somewhere. A dear, pale, sorrowful shade which I must never disturb. Margot? No, this brother-and-sister state of things is only for the time being. What is it then?"

Without quite knowing what he wanted, he crept out of bed and groped his way to Margot's door (his room had no other exit). She always locked it at night and so he was shut in.

"How wise she is," he thought tenderly, and he put his ear to the keyhole, hoping to hear her breathing in her sleep. But he heard nothing.

"Quiet as a little mouse," he whispered. "If I could just stroke her head and then go away. Perhaps she has forgotten to lock the door."

Without much hope he pressed the latch. No, she had not forgotten.

He suddenly remembered how, one sultry summer night when he was a pimply youth, he had clambered along the cornice of a house on the Rhine from his room into that of the housemaid (only to find that she was not sleeping alone) —

but at that time he was light and nimble; at that time he could see.

"Still, why should I not try?" he thought with melancholy daring. "And if I do fall and break my neck, will it matter?"

First he found his stick, leaned out of the window and groped with it to the left over the sill to the neighboring window. It was open and the pane tinkled as the stick touched it.

"How fast asleep she is!" he thought. "Must be exhausting, looking after me all day long."

As he drew back the stick he caught it on something. It slipped from his grasp and fell to the ground below with a faint thud.

Albinus held onto the window frame, clambered out onto the sill, made his way to the left along the cornice, clutching at what was presumably the water-pipe, stepped across its cold iron bend and clutched the window sill of the next room.

"How simple!" he thought, not without pride, and "Hello, Margot," he said, softly, trying to crawl in through the open window. He slipped and almost fell backward into the abstraction of a garden. His heart was beating violently. He wriggled over the sill into the room and some heavy object which he displaced fell to the ground noisily.

He stood still. His face was covered with sweat. On his hand he felt something sticky (it was resin which had oozed out of the pine-wood of which the house was built).

"Margot, darling," he said cheerfully. Silence. He found the bed. It was covered with a lace spread—had not been slept in.

Albinus seated himself on it and reflected. If the bed had been open and warm, then it would have been easy to understand, she would be back in a moment.

After a few moments he went out into the corridor (much hampered by the absence of his stick) and listened. He fancied that he heard somewhere a low smothered sound—something between a creak and a rustle. It began to be uncanny. He called out:

"Margot, where are you?"

Everything remained silent. Then a door opened.

"Margot, Margot," he repeated, groping his way down the corridor.

"Yes, yes, I'm here," her voice answered calmly.

"What's happened, Margot? Why haven't you gone to bed?"

She collided with him in the dark passage and

when he touched her he felt that she was undressed.

"I was lying in the sun," she said, "as I always
do in the morning."

"But now it's night," he exclaimed, breathing
heavily. "I can't understand. There's something
wrong somewhere. I know because I felt the
hands of the clock. It's half past one."

"Rubbish. It's half past six and a lovely sunny
morning. Your clock must have gone wrong. You
feel the hands too often. But look here—how did
you get out of your room?"

"Margot, is it really morning? Are you telling
the truth?"

She suddenly went close up to him and, standing on tiptoe, laid her arms round his neck as she
had done in the old days.

"Although it's day," she said softly, "if you
like, if you like, dearest . . . As a great exception . . ."

She did not much want to do it, but it was the
only way. Now Albinus could no longer notice
that the air was still cold, and that no birds were
singing, for he felt only one thing—fierce, fiery
bliss, and then he sank into a deep sleep and slept
until midday. When he woke up Margot scolded
him for his climbing exploit, was still more furi-

ous when she saw his melancholy smile, and slapped his cheek.

The whole of that day he sat in the drawing room, thinking of his happy morning and wondering how many days it would be before this happiness would be repeated. All of a sudden, quite distinctly, he heard someone emit a dubious little cough. That could not be Margot. He knew she was in the kitchen.

"Who's there?" he asked.

But no one answered.

"Another hallucination!" thought Albinus wearily and then, all at once, he understood what it was that had worried him so at night—yes, yes, it was these strange noises which he sometimes heard.

"Tell me, Margot," he said, as she came back, "is there no one in the house besides Emilia? Are you quite sure?"

"You nut!" she answered curtly.

But once the suspicion had been aroused, it refused to give him any rest. He sat still all day and listened gloomily.

Rex was very much amused at this, and although Margot had besought him to be more prudent, he paid no heed to her warning. Once even, when he was only two feet away from Albinus, he very skilfully began to whistle like an

* of Gaslight !

oriole. Margot had to explain that the bird had perched on the window sill and was singing there.

"Drive it away," said Albinus sternly.

"Ssh, ssh," said Margot, laying her hand on Rex's fat lips.

"Do you know," said Albinus a few days later, "I should like to have a chat with Emilia. I like her puddings."

"Absolutely out of the question," answered Margot. "She is quite deaf and mortally afraid of you."

Albinus thought hard for some minutes.

"Impossible," he said slowly.

"What's impossible, Albert?"

"Oh, nothing," he muttered, "nothing."

"Do you know, Margot," he said shortly afterward, "I'm badly in need of a shave. Send for the hairdresser from the village."

"Unnecessary," said Margot. "The beard suits you very well."

Albinus fancied that someone—not Margot, but someone by the side of Margot—tittered softly.

~§ 37 §~

THE *Berliner Zeitung*, with a brief account of
the accident, was shown to Paul by a man in his
office, and he at once drove home, fearing that
Elisabeth had read it, too. She had not, though
curiously enough a copy of that particular paper
(which they did not usually read) was in the
house. He wired the same day to the Grasse
police station and eventually got into touch with
the hospital doctor, who replied, saying that Albinus was out of danger, but quite blind. Very
gently he broke the news to Elisabeth.

Then, owing to the simple fact that he and his
brother-in-law both had the same bank, he discovered Albinus' address in Switzerland. The
manager, an old business friend of his, showed
him the checks that were pouring in from there
with a kind of hasty regularity, and Paul was
amazed at the amount of cash Albinus was drawing out. The signature was all right, though very

shaky about the curves and pathetically down-sloping, but the figures were written in another hand—a bold masculine hand with a dash and a flourish, and there was somehow a faint whiff of forgery about the whole thing. He wondered whether it was the fact of the blind man signing what he was told, and not what he saw, that created this queer impression. Queer, too, were the large sums he demanded—as if he, or somebody else, were in a frantic hurry to get out as much money as he could. And then came a check that was uncovered.

"There's some foul business going on," thought Paul, "I feel it in my bones. But what is it exactly?"

He pictured to himself Albinus, alone with his dangerous mistress, completely at her mercy, in the black house of his blindness . . .

Some days passed. Paul was dreadfully un-easy. It was not the mere fact of the man signing checks he could not see (anyway, the money was his to squander consciously or unconsciously—Elisabeth did not need it and there was no longer any Irma to be thought about), but the fact of his being so utterly helpless in the wicked world that he had let grow up around him.

One evening, as Paul came home, he found Elisabeth packing a portmanteau. It was curious that she looked happier than she had done for many months.

"What's up?" he asked. "Are you going any- where?"

"You are," she said quietly.

◄§ 38 ৪►

THE next day Paul traveled to Switzerland. At Brigaud he took a taxi, and in something over an hour reached the little town above which Albinus was living. Paul stopped in front of the post office and a very talkative young woman in charge of the latter told him the way to the chalet and added that Albinus was staying there with his niece and a doctor. Paul drove on immediately. He knew who the niece was. But the presence of a doctor surprised him. It seemed to suggest that Albinus was being better looked after than might be supposed.

"Perhaps, after all, I've come here on a fool's errand," thought Paul uncomfortably. "He may be quite contented. But now that I'm here . . . Well, anyway, I'll have a talk with this doctor. Poor fellow, a shattered life . . . Who could have thought . . ."

That morning Margot had gone to the village

with Emilia. She did not notice Paul's taxi; but at the post office she was told that a stout gentleman had just inquired after Albinus and had driven on up to see him.

At this moment Albinus and Rex were seated opposite one another in the little drawing room into which the sunlight was streaming through the glass door leading to the terrace. Rex sat on a folding stool. He was stark naked. As a result of his daily sunbaths his lean but robust body with, on his breast, black hair in the shape of a spread eagle, was tanned a deep brown. Between his full red lips he held a long stalk of grass and, with his hairy legs crossed and his chin cupped in his hand (rather in the pose of Rodin's "Thinker") he was staring at Albinus who, in return, seemed to be gazing at him quite as intently.

The blind man was wearing an ample, mouse-gray dressing-gown and his bearded face expressed agonized tension. He was listening—of late he had done nothing else but listen. Rex knew this and was watching how the man's thoughts were mirrored on his face as if that face had become one big eye since his actual pair of eyes had gone. One or two little tests might add to the fun: he slapped his knee softly, and Albinus, who had just raised his hand to his knitted

276

brow, remained transfixed with uplifted arm.
Then Rex bent slowly forward and touched Albinus' forehead very gently with the flowering
end of the grass stem which he had just been
sucking. Albinus sighed strangely and brushed
away the imaginary fly. Rex tickled his lips and
again Albinus made that helpless movement.
This was good fun indeed.

Suddenly the blind man cocked his head
abruptly. Rex, too, turned and through the glass
door he saw a stout gentleman in a checkered
cap whose red face he recognized at once and
who was standing there, on the terrace, and looking on in amazement.

Rex put his finger to his lips and made a sign
to him, meaning that he would join him in a moment. But the other pushed open the door and
stepped into the room.

"Of course, I know you. Your name is Rex,"
said Paul, taking a deep breath and staring at
this naked man who still smiled and held his
finger to his lips.

Albinus had meanwhile risen to his feet. The
reddish hue of his scar seemed to have spread
over his whole forehead. Suddenly he began to
scream and jabber and only gradually words
formed themselves out of these jagged sounds.

"Paul, I'm here alone," he cried. "Paul, do say

that I'm alone. That man is in America. He is not here. Paul, I implore you. I'm quite blind."

"Pity you've spoiled everything," said Rex, and then he ran out and began mounting the stairs.

Paul seized the blind man's stick, caught up with Rex, who turned round and held up his hands to protect himself; and Paul, good-natured Paul who had never in his life hit a living creature, swung out mightily at Rex's head and got it with a tremendous bang. Rex leaped back—his face still twisted in a smile—and suddenly something very remarkable occurred: like Adam after the Fall, Rex, cowering by the white wall and grinning wanly, covered his nakedness with his hand.

Paul rushed after him again, but the man dodged and ran up the steps.

At this moment someone fell upon Paul from behind. It was Albinus—clutching, whimpering and holding a marble letter-weight in his hand.

"Paul," he groaned, "Paul, I understand everything. Give me my overcoat, quick. It's hanging in the wardrobe there."

"Which—the yellow one?" asked Paul, struggling for breath.

Albinus immediately felt what he wanted in the pocket, and he stopped blubbering.

"I'll take you away from here at once," panted Paul. "Take off your dressing-gown and put on that coat. Give me that letter-weight. Come on. I'll help you . . . There, take my cap. It doesn't matter that you've only got bedroom slippers on. Let's get away, let's get away, Albert. I've got a taxi down there. The first thing to be done is to get you out of this torture chamber."

"Wait a bit," said Albinus. "I must speak to her first. She will be back in a moment. I must, Paul. It won't take long."

But Paul pushed him out into the garden and then shouted and beckoned to the chauffeur.

"I must speak to her," repeated Albinus. "Quite close. For God's sake, Paul, tell me, perhaps she's here already? Perhaps she's come back?"

"No, calm yourself. We must go. There's no one here. Only that naked wretch looking out of the window. Come on, Albert, come on!"

"Yes, we'll go," said Albinus, "but you must tell me if you see her. We may meet her on the way. Then I must speak to her. Quite close, quite close."

They went down the footpath, but after a few steps Albinus suddenly opened his arms and fell back in a swoon. The taxi driver came hurrying up and together they lifted Albinus into the car.

One of his slippers remained there on the footpath.

At that moment a trap drove up and Margot jumped out of it. She ran toward them and shouted something, but the car was already turning in the road; it almost knocked her down as it backed, then it lurched forward and disappeared round the bend.

❧ 39 ❧

ON TUESDAY Elisabeth received a telegram and at about eight on Wednesday night she heard Paul's voice in the hall and the pat-pat of a stick. The door opened and Paul led in her husband. *now*

He was clean-shaven; he was wearing dark spectacles; there was a scar on his pale forehead. The unfamiliar purplish brown suit (a shade he would never have chosen himself) seemed rather too large for him.

"Here he is," said Paul quietly.

Elisabeth began to sob, pressing her handkerchief to her mouth. Albinus bowed silently in the direction of the smothered sobbing.

"Come along, we'll wash our hands," said Paul, leading him slowly across the room.

Then the three of them sat in the dining room and had supper. Elisabeth had difficulty in accustoming herself to look at her husband. It

281

seemed to her that he felt her glance. The melancholy gravity of his slow movements filled her with a tranquil ecstasy of pity. Paul talked to him as though he were a child, and cut up the ham on his plate into little pieces.

He was given what had been Irma's nursery. It surprised Elisabeth that she found it so easy to disturb the sacred slumber of that little room for the sake of this strange, large, silent occupant; to shift and change all its contents so as to adapt it to the blind man's needs.

Albinus said nothing. At first, to be sure—while they were still in Switzerland—he had begged Paul with petulant persistency to ask Margot to come and see him; he had sworn that this final meeting would not last more than a moment. (And, indeed, would it take long to grope in the wonted darkness and, holding her tightly with one hand, to thrust the barrel of the automatic against her side and to stuff her with bullets?) Paul had obstinately refused to do as he asked, and after that Albinus had said nothing. He traveled to Berlin in silence, he arrived in silence and he was silent for the next three days, so that Elisabeth never heard his voice any more (except perhaps once): he might have been dumb as well as blind.

The heavy black object, the treasure-house of

282

seven compressed deaths, lay wrapped in his silk muffler in the depths of his overcoat pocket. Then, when he arrived, he managed to transfer it to a chest of drawers near his bed. He kept the key in his waistcoat pocket and put it under his pillow at night. Once or twice they noticed that he was fumbling and clutching something in his hand, but no comments were made. The touch of that key against his palm, its slight weight in his pocket, seemed to him a kind of Sesame that would—he was certain of it—one day unlock the door of his blindness.

And he still said not a word. Elisabeth's presence, her light tread, her whispering (she always spoke to the servants and to Paul in a whisper now, as if there were great sickness in the house) were just as pale and shadowy as was his memory of her: an almost soundless memory drifting about listlessly with a faint trail of eau-de-Cologne —that was all. Real life, which was cruel, supple and strong like some anaconda, and which he longed to destroy without delay, was somewhere else—but where? He did not know. With extraordinary distinctness he pictured Margot and Rex—both quick and alert, with terrible, beaming, goggle eyes and long, lithe limbs—packing after his departure; Margot fawned, and caressed Rex among the open trunks and then they both went away—but where, where? Not a light in the darkness. But their sinuous path burned in him like the trace which a foul, crawling creature leaves on the skin.

Three silent days passed. On the fourth, early in the morning, it so happened that Albinus was alone. Paul had just gone to the police (there were certain things which he wanted to elucidate), the maid was in a back room and Elisabeth, who had not slept all night, was not yet up. Albinus wandered about in an agony of restlessness, fingering the furniture and the doors. For some time the telephone had been ringing in the study, and this reminded him that there was, by this means, the possibility of getting certain information: someone might tell him whether the artist Rex was back in Berlin. But he could not remember a single telephone number and he knew moreover that he would not be able to pronounce that name in spite of its shortness. The ringing became more and more insistent. Albinus found his way to the table, took up the invisible receiver . . .

A voice which seemed to him familiar asked for Herr Hochenwart—that is, for Paul.

"He is out," answered Albinus.

The voice hesitated, then suddenly exclaimed brightly:

"Why, is it you, Herr Albinus?"

"Yes. And who are you?"

"Schiffermiller. I just rang up Herr Hochenwart's office, but he had not arrived. So I thought I'd get him here. How lucky my getting you, Herr Albinus!"

"What's the matter?" asked Albinus.

"Well, probably it's quite all right, but I thought my duty was to make quite sure. You see, Fräulein Peters has just come to fetch some things, and . . . well . . . I let her into your flat, but I don't quite know . . . So I thought I'd better . . ."

"That's all right," said Albinus, moving his lips with difficulty (they felt numb as though from cocaine).

"What did you say, Herr Albinus?"

Albinus made a great effort to conquer speech: "That's all right," he repeated distinctly, and hung up with a trembling hand.

He blundered back into his room, unlocked the sacred chest, then went, groping, into the hall and tried to find his hat and stick. But that took too long and he gave it up. Cautiously he patted and shuffled his way down the stairs, clutching the banisters and muttering to himself feverishly. In a few moments he was standing in the street. Something cold and tickling was dripping on his

285

forehead: rain. He held onto the iron railing of the front garden and desperately prayed for the sound of a taxi-horn. Soon he heard the moist, leisurely swish of tires. He shouted, but the sound moved away unheedingly.

"May I help you across?" asked a pleasant young voice.

"For heaven's sake, get me a cab," implored Albinus.

Once more the sound of tires approached. Someone helped him into the taxi and slammed the door. (A window opened in the fourth story, but it was too late.)

"Straight ahead, straight ahead," said Albinus softly, and, when the taxi was once in motion, he tapped with his finger on the glass and gave the address.

"I'll count the turnings," thought Albinus. The first one—this will be Motzstrasse. To the left he heard the shrill jingle of an electric tram. Albinus passed his hand over the seat, the front partition and the floor, suddenly disquieted by the thought that someone might be sitting beside him. Another turning. This must be the Victoria-Luisenplatz or the Pragerplatz? In a moment he would be at the Kaiserallee.

The taxi stopped. Am I really there already? It can't be. It's only a cross-road. It must be at least another five minutes . . . But the door opened.

"This is number fifty-six," said the taxi driver.

Albinus stepped out of the taxi. Through the air in front of him arose cheerfully a complete edition of the voice which he had just heard on the telephone. Schiffermiller, the house-porter, said:

"Glad to see you again, Herr Albinus. The young lady is upstairs, in your flat. She . . ."

"Hush, hush," whispered Albinus, "pay the taxi, please. My eyes are . . ."

His knee hit against something which wobbled and jingled—probably a child's bicycle on the pavement.

"Lead me into the house," he said. "Give me the key of my flat. Quick, please. And now take me to the lift. No, no, you can stay downstairs. I'll go up alone. I'll press the button myself."

The lift made a low, moaning sound and he felt a faint dizziness. Then the floor seemed to jerk against the soles of his felt slippers. He had arrived.

He got out of the lift, moved forward and stepped with one foot into an abyss—no, it was nothing, only the step leading downstairs. He had to keep still for a moment, he was quivering so.

"It's to the right, more to the right," he whispered, and, with outstretched hand, he walked across the landing. At last he found the keyhole, thrust in the key and turned it.

Ah, there it was, the sound he had coveted for days—just to the left, in the little drawing room . . . a crackle of wrapping paper and then a soft creaking like the sound made by the joints of a person who is crouching down.

"I shall want you in a minute, Herr Schiffermiller," said Margot's strained voice. "You must help me to carry this thing . . ."

The voice broke off.

"She has seen me," thought Albinus, drawing the pistol out of his pocket.

To the left, in the drawing room, he heard the click of a valise-lock closing. Margot gave a little grunt of satisfaction—it had closed after all—and continued in a sing-song tone:

". . . to carry this down. Or perhaps you might call . . ."

At the word "call" her voice seemed to turn round and suddenly it was silent.

Albinus was holding the pistol in his right hand ready for use, while with his left he felt the post of the open door, entered, slammed the door behind him and stood with his back to it.

Everything was quiet. But he knew that he

was alone with Margot in the room and that this room had only one exit—the one he was blocking. He could see the room distinctly—almost as if he had the use of his eyes: to the left, the striped sofa, against the right wall, a small table with the porcelain figure of a ballet-dancer; in the corner by the window, the cabinet with the valuable miniatures; in the middle, another large table, very shiny and smooth.

Albinus stretched out his fist and moved the gun slowly to and fro, trying to induce some sound which would betray her exact position. He felt that she was somewhere near the miniatures; from that direction he could catch a faint whiff of warmth tinged with the perfume called "*L'heure bleue*"; in that corner something was trembling like the air above sand on a very hot day by the sea. He narrowed the curve along which his hand traveled and suddenly he heard a faint rustle. Shoot? No, not yet. He must get much nearer to her. He knocked against the middle table and came to a standstill. He felt that Margot was stealing to one side, but his own body, though fairly still, made so much noise that he could not hear her. Yes, now she was more to the left, near the window. Oh, if she lost her head and started opening it and shrieking, that would be divine—he would have a lovely target.

But what if she slid past him round the table as he advanced? "Better lock the door," he thought. No, there was no key (doors were always against him). He gripped the edge of the table with one hand and, stepping backward, pulled it toward the door so as to have it behind him. Again the warmth he sensed shifted, shrank, diminished. Having blocked up the exit, he felt freer and again, with the point of his pistol, he located a living, quivering something in the darkness.

Now he advanced as quietly as possible so that he might detect every sound. Blind man's buff, blind man's buff . . . in a country-house on a winter night, long, long ago. He stumbled against something hard and felt it with one hand, never for a moment letting loose the line which he held taut across the room. It was a small trunk. He thrust it away with his knee and moved on, driving the invisible prey before him into an imaginary corner. Her silence irritated him at first; but now he could detect her quite plainly. It was not her breathing, not the beating of her heart, but a sort of general impression: the voice of her life itself, which, in another moment, he would destroy. And then—peace, serenity, light.

Suddenly he was conscious of a relaxation of tension in the corner before him. He shifted the gun, and forced her warm presence back again.

It seemed, that presence, to bend all at once as a flame in a draft; then it crawled, stretched . . . was coming at his legs. Albinus could control himself no longer; with a fierce groan he pressed the trigger.

The shot rent the darkness, and immediately afterward something struck him across the knees, bringing him down, and for a second he was entangled in a chair that had been flung at him. As he fell he dropped the pistol, but found it again at once. At the same time he was conscious of rapid breathing, a smell of scent and sweat hit his nostrils, and a cold, nimble hand tried to wrench the weapon from his grasp. Albinus seized something living, something that let forth a hideous cry, as though a nightmare creature were being tickled by its nightmare mate. The hand he was catching twisted the pistol free and he felt the barrel prod him; and, together with a faint detonation that seemed miles away, in another world, there came a stab in his side which filled his eyes with a dazzling glory.

"So that's all," he thought quite softly, as if he were lying in bed. "I must keep quiet for a little space and then walk very slowly along that bright sand of pain, toward that blue, blue wave. What bliss there is in blueness. I never knew how blue blueness could be. What a mess life has been.

Now I know everything. Coming, coming, coming to drown me. There it is. How it hurts. I can't breathe . . ."

He sat on the floor with bowed head, then bent slowly forward and fell, like a big, soft doll, to one side.

Stage-directions for last silent scene: door—wide open. Table—thrust away from it. Carpet—bulging up at table foot in a frozen wave. Chair—lying close by dead body of man in a purplish brown suit and felt slippers. Automatic pistol not visible. It is under him. Cabinet where the miniatures had been—empty. On the other (small) table, on which ages ago a porcelain ballet-dancer stood (later transferred to another room) lies a woman's glove, black outside, white inside. By the striped sofa stands a smart little trunk, with a colored label still adhering to it: "Rouginard, Hôtel Britannia."

The door leading from the hall to the landing is wide open, too.

THE END

New Directions Paperbooks – A Partial Listing

For complete listing request free catalog from
New Directions, 80 Eighth Avenue, New York 10011

† Bilingual

The Smile at the Foot of the Ladder. NDP386.
  Stand Still Like the Hummingbird. NDP236.
  The Time of the Assassins. NDP115.
Y. Mishima, Confessions of a Mask. NDP253.
  Death in Midsummer. NDP215.
Frédéric Mistral, The Memoirs. NDP632.
Eugenio Montale, It Depends.† NDP507.
  New Poems. NDP410.
  Selected Poems.† NDP193.
Paul Morand, Fancy Goods/Open All Night.
  NDP567.
Vladimir Nabokov, Nikolai Gogol. NDP78.
  Laughter in the Dark. NDP470.
  The Real Life of Sebastian Knight. NDP432.
P. Neruda, The Captain's Verses.† NDP345.
  Residence on Earth.† NDP340.
New Directions in Prose & Poetry (Anthology).
  Available from #17 forward to #52.
Robert Nichols, Arrival. NDP437.
  Exile. NDP485. Garh City. NDP450.
  Harditts in Sawna. NDP470.
Charles Olson, Selected Writings. NDP231.
Toby Olson, The Life of Jesus. NDP417.
  Seaview. NDP532.
George Oppen, Collected Poems. NDP418.
István Örkeny, The Flower Show /
  The Toth Family. NDP536.
Wilfred Owen, Collected Poems. NDP210.
José Emilio Pacheco, Battles in the Desert, NDP637.
  Selected Poems.† NDP638.
Nicanor Parra, Antipoems: New & Selected. NDP603.
Boris Pasternak, Safe Conduct. NDP77.
Kenneth Patchen, Aflame and Afun. NDP292.
  Because It Is. NDP83.
  Collected Poems. NDP284.
  Hallelujah Anyway. NDP219.
  Selected Poems. NDP160.
Octavio Paz, Configurations.† NDP303.
  A Draft of Shadows.† NDP489.
  Eagle or Sun?† NDP422.
  Selected Poems. NDP574.
  A Tree Within,† NDP661.
St. John Perse. Selected Poems.† NDP545.
J. A. Porter, Eelgrass. NDP438.
Ezra Pound, ABC of Reading. NDP89.
  Confucius. NDP285.
  Confucius to Cummings. (Anth.) NDP126.
  Gaudier Brzeska. NDP372.
  Guide to Kulchur. NDP257.
  Literary Essays. NDP250.
  Selected Cantos. NDP304.
  Selected Letters 1907-1941. NDP317.
  Selected Poems. NDP66.
  The Spirit of Romance. NDP266.
  Translations.† (Enlarged Edition) NDP145.
  Women of Trachis. NDP597.
Raymond Queneau, The Blue Flowers. NDP595.
  Exercises in Style. NDP513.
  The Sunday of Life. NDP433.
Mary de Rachewiltz, Ezra Pound. NDP405.
Raja Rao, Kanthapura. NDP224.
Herbert Read, The Green Child. NDP208.
P. Reverdy, Selected Poems.† NDP346.
Kenneth Rexroth, Classics Revisited. NDP621.
  More Classics Revisited, NDP668.
  100 More Poems from the Chinese. NDP308.
  100 More Poems from the Japanese.† NDP420.
  100 Poems from the Chinese. NDP192.
  100 Poems from the Japanese.† NDP147.
  Selected Poems. NDP581.
  Women Poets of China. NDP528.
  Women Poets of Japan. NDP527.
  World Outside the Window, Sel. Essays, NDP639.
Rainer Maria Rilke, Poems from
  The Book of Hours. NDP408.
  Possibility of Being. (Poems). NDP436.
  Where Silence Reigns. (Prose). NDP464.
Arthur Rimbaud, Illuminations.† NDP56.
  Season in Hell & Drunken Boat.† NDP97.
Edouard Roditi, Delights of Turkey. NDP445.

Oscar Wilde. NDP624.
Jerome Rothenberg, New Selected Poems. NDP625.
Nayantara Sahgal, Rich Like Us, NDP665.
Saigyo, Mirror for the Moon.† NDP465.
Ihara Saikaku, The Life of an Amorous
  Woman. NDP270.
St. John of the Cross, Poems.† NDP341.
Jean-Paul Sartre, Nausea. NDP82.
  The Wall (Intimacy). NDP272.
Delmore Schwartz, Selected Poems. NDP241.
  The Ego Is Always at the Wheel, NDP641.
  In Dreams Begin Responsibilities. NDP454.
Stevie Smith, Collected Poems. NDP562.
  New Selected Poems, NDP659.
Gary Snyder, The Back Country. NDP249.
  The Real Work. NDP499.
  Regarding Wave. NDP306.
  Turtle Island. NDP381.
Enid Starkie, Rimbaud. NDP254.
Robert Steiner, Bathers. NDP495.
Antonio Tabucchi, Letter from Casablanca. NDP620.
Nathaniel Tarn, Lyrics . . . Bride of God. NDP391.
Dylan Thomas, Adventures in the Skin Trade.
  NDP183.
  A Child's Christmas in Wales. NDP181.
  Collected Poems 1934-1952. NDP316.
  Collected Stories. NDP626.
  Portrait of the Artist as a Young Dog. NDP51.
  Quite Early One Morning. NDP90.
  Under Milk Wood. NDP73.
Tian Wen: A Chinese Book of Origins. NDP624.
Lionel Trilling, E. M. Forster. NDP189.
Martin Turnell, Baudelaire. NDP336.
  Rise of the French Novel. NDP474.
Paul Valéry, Selected Writings.† NDP184.
Elio Vittorini, A Vittorini Omnibus. NDP366.
Rosmarie Waldrop, The Reproduction of Profiles,
  NDP649.
Robert Penn Warren, At Heaven's Gate. NDP588.
Vernon Watkins, Selected Poems. NDP221.
Weinberger, Eliot, Works on Paper. NDP627.
Nathanael West, Miss Lonelyhearts &
  Day of the Locust. NDP125.
J. Wheelwright, Collected Poems. NDP544.
Tennessee Williams, Camino Real. NDP301.
  Cat on a Hot Tin Roof. NDP398.
  Clothes for a Summer Hotel. NDP556.
  The Glass Menagerie. NDP218.
  Hard Candy. NDP225.
  In the Winter of Cities. NDP154.
  A Lovely Sunday for Creve Coeur. NDP497.
  One Arm & Other Stories. NDP237.
  Stopped Rocking. NDP575.
  A Streetcar Named Desire. NDP501.
  Sweet Bird of Youth. NDP409.
  Twenty-Seven Wagons Full of Cotton. NDP217.
  Vieux Carre. NDP482.
William Carlos Williams,
  The Autobiography. NDP223.
  The Buildup. NDP259.
  The Doctor Stories. NDP585.
  Imaginations. NDP329.
  In the American Grain. NDP53.
  In the Money. NDP240.
  Paterson. Complete. NDP152.
  Pictures form Brueghel. NDP118.
  Selected Letters. NDP589.
  Selected Poems (new ed.). NDP602.
  White Mule. NDP226.
  Yes, Mrs. Williams. NDP534.
Yvor Winters, E. A. Robinson. NDP326.
Wisdom Books: Ancient Egyptians.NDP467.
  Early Buddhists, NDP444; Forest (Hindu).
  NDP414; Spanish Mystics. NDP442; St. Francis.
  NDP477; Taoists. NDP509; Wisdom of the Desert.
  NDP295; Zen Masters. NDP415.

For complete listing request free catalog from
New Directions, 80 Eighth Avenue, New York 10011   † Bilingual